DARK SWIRL

DARK SWIRL

CYRIL DABYDEEN

PEEPAL TREE

First published in Great Britain in 1989
Reprinted in 2007
Peepal Tree Press Ltd
17 King's Avenue
Leeds LS6 1QS
England

ISBN 0 948833 20 3
ISBN 13: 9780948833205

Peepal Tree gratefully acknowledges Arts Council support

Thanks to Gerald Durrell for his wonderful stories about animals, which I first began reading in my early teens. The stories about the tropics, in particular, inspired my greater appreciation for the animal life that is so abundant in the rivers and creeks of my native Guyana.

For Claire, Leonard, David, Stanley, Fred, Frank, Hassan, Slim, Sal & the others (and most especially, Jeremy, for being himself as well as being the best editor a writer can have).

I listen to the song jarring my mouth
Where the skull-rooted teeth are in possession.
I am massive on earth. My feetbones beat on the earth
Over the sounds of motherly weeping...

Afterwards I drink at a pool quietly.
The horizon bears the rocks and trees away into twilight.
I lie down. I become darkness.

Darkness that all night sings and circles stamping.

'Gog', Ted Hughes
Selected Poems, 1957-1967

The fish had in its mouth two different things of which one
must go into the stomach and the other into the nest. What
would he do? I must confess that, at that moment, I would
not have given twopence for the life of that tiny jewel fish.
But wonderful what really happened! The fish stood stock
still with full cheeks, but did not chew. If ever I have seen
a fish think, it was in that moment!

Konrad Lorenz, *King Soloman's Ring*

ONE

The water in the creek glistened, darkly. Sometimes it had the colour of coffee, sometimes chocolate. Even the vegetation which clogged up the bottom was dark, which was why it was impossible to see beneath the surface.

Josh stood at his familiar spot by the window, staring out over the creek, unable to look away, wishing the water was clear enough to see exactly what was at the bottom. Closing his eyes, he imagined things swimming under the surface: the fish, the alligators, other reptiles. He did this day after day. When he sensed a sudden movement he looked closer but could see nothing. Now he wished that rain would fall, for the rhythm of the heavy drops both excited him and soothed his mind.

But the water still glistened darkly. No rains came. Again he imagined fish swimming under the surface, swimming back and forth, some in perpetual frenzy.

He imagined ferocious fish, like the perai, devouring smaller fish like the tilapia. He winced. There were other things in the creek: reptiles and strange-looking crustaceans. He imagined them raising their ugly heads to look at him. Sometimes he felt they were playing a game.

He remained by the window for hours. Now and again his eyes strayed beyond the creek: to the houses, to the lush sugarcane fields, to the widening horizon: a different world altogether. But he always looked back into the creek, familiar ground.

For a moment he looked up at the sun. Squinting, he watched it decline, bright vermilion, dark russet. The colours remained in his mind, a contrast to the dark water which, when he looked into it again, seemed more actively alive than usual. He pursed his lips as he felt a tremor in his veins, felt unlike himself.

'Josh, whe' you gone?' his mother called. He was one of her many children.

'He gone by heself again,' answered a brother.

Everyone wondered about Josh, because of his strange habit. He was aged ten, somewhere in the middle amongst the children, but his mother treated him as if he was the youngest.

'Go an' see if he deh next the window,' she said, sighing.

'He lookin' at the creek again,' said the younger voice, about to scoff.

'That chile...' she murmured to herself. 'He in' like the rest o' them.' She scratched the fine jet-black hair on her forearms. 'Maybe he know t'ings 'bout dat creek that none of the rest o' we know.' Like almost everyone else in the village she had her suspicions. Nearly everyone, at one time or another, had imagined strange reptiles crawling out of the creek at nights and inhabiting the space under their beds, or even crawling into the beds and lying next to them. She had dreamt of alligators crawling out from the thick brush and entering the house to sleep comfortably in a corner. Once, too, she had dreamt of the massacouraman. A giddiness swept over her as images of this thing, so changeable, with so many faces, passed through her mind.

But these thoughts never lasted long. In her forty-two years she'd never seen a live alligator close-up, only the ones killed by the menfolk and left lying stretched out on the road. Even then no dead alligator ever remained for long on the bank. Though no one had witnessed it, villagers were sure that other reptiles came out of the creek late at night and carried the dead one back into the water.

Josh appeared with his older brother. 'Whe' you been?' asked his mother. Josh didn't answer.

'Nex' the window – where else?' his brother replied, snickering.

'Wha' you do deh?' she asked out of habit. She knew Josh wouldn't say; he'd just lower his head, as if he had a strange secret to keep. One day she hoped Josh would say something that would make her rush to tell her husband; then all the neighbours.

'Yuh got to tell me,' she urged. 'Tell me what you seeing in the creek.'

Josh's brother laughed. 'He just playing de ass – tha's all!' He grinned and wiped a spittle-stained mouth with the back of his hand.

Josh looked furtively at his brother, then at his mother. She stared expectantly.

Josh lowered his head once more.

'He in talkin' at all,' sighed his brother.

'He might talk,' she muttered, coaxing.

'He might tell de whiteman,' suggested the brother, teasing.

His mother looked surprised. 'He won' do that.'

Everyone in the village was curious about the white man. He was always peering into the odd places at the edge of the creek; a strange-looking man, with mottled white skin, a shaggy head of knotted blonde hair, his face fringed by a thick beard. He had looked alarming at first, but now everyone was getting used to seeing him.

'Come an' eat,' his mother said.

Josh reluctantly followed her.

He sat on the floor with the others. A plate of fish and rice was put before him. He looked at it, then at the others eating. He picked at his food slowly, fingering the head of the fish, a *basha,* with part of the neck attached to it. He looked at the fish's eyes; one dead eye seemed to stare back at him.

Inwardly he shuddered.

'Eat!' his mother urged.

Josh picked at the neck, putting a morsel into his mouth. He swallowed quickly, and felt the fish going down his throat with the grains of rice. He hiccoughed.

The others, watching him, laughed.

'Don' laugh at he!' his mother chided; she wanted Josh to continue eating since he was thin, much thinner than other boys his age.

Josh was now afraid to put another morsel into his mouth. He hiccoughed again.

The others giggled.

His father looked at him, then at the others. At home he was a silent man, much given to thought. He left most of the talking to his wife. Suddenly he let out, 'Stop na! All yuh stop dat – right away!'

Josh feared his father's voice, especially when it rose like this. Slowly now, because he knew his father was looking at him, he put another morsel into his mouth and stifled his hiccough. He chewed the fish and swallowed hard. He put another, then another, swallowing rapidly now. The others were also eating, racing to see who would finish first.

Josh looked up; first at his father, then at his mother. He saw them looking pleased. He lowered his eyes once more, to his own plate which was almost finished now.

'It fatten you,' his mother said, smiling. 'Fish – mek yuh grow good – all o' you!'

His father said nothing. He merely rubbed a hand across the side of his brown face as if this said all he wanted to say.

Josh got up and went to the sink to wash his hands. The others followed behind in line giggling, but their father's admonishing glare cut that short.

Later that evening Josh returned to the window. The sun had gone down completely. He looked at the meadow beyond the creek, watching the cows ambling along to the cow-pens, like huge shadows.

He turned his gaze to the creek, studying each ripple, wondering what kind of fish it could be under the surface. A ripple widened. Josh looked more keenly, straining his neck forward. He imagined a big fish chasing a smaller one. He was about to wince, but then he thought of two fish playing, just as his brothers and sisters did...

Next he noticed more ripples among the scattered mucka-mucka vegetation. He looked to the far corner; there was something bigger, a dark head, eyes that seemed to blink back at him, an alligator perhaps, but bigger than he'd ever seen or heard about. Then slowly the head submerged, the ripples disappearing. It was deathly quiet.

He waited. Above, clouds slowly drifted, darkening. A cow mooed loudly. Somewhere a parakeet screeched, then a splash in the water, some distance from him. But Josh heard it nevertheless. He suddenly imagined a huge commotion with ever widening ripples extending as far as the bank, coming closer to him. He could feel it wetting him, blinding him. He closed his eyes and braced himself for the tremor about to engulf him.

'Josh!' a voice called out.

He turned around, still frightened.

He saw his brother grinning. 'Wha' happening, Josh? Wha' you see?'

He didn't answer.

'You dreamin'? Like yuh see jumbie. You hand tremble!'

Still he didn't answer.

'Tell me, Josh!' The brother looked into the creek over his shoulder. He saw nothing, only the blackness. He was about to laugh but the look on Josh's face made him stop.

Later that night in bed, Josh kept thinking about the ripple. He was afraid to close his eyes, thinking it would suddenly

13

appear like a giant wave and overwhelm him. He imagined the wave with a face, a strange hideous creature.

Even when Josh heard his brothers snoring heavily, he was still awake.

Then the rains came; loud, heavy drops falling on the galvanised zinc-topped roof of the house. The pitter-patter kept him alert for a while. He opened and closed his eyes, thinking, not sure about what. It was as if the raindrops were falling on him; he would drown.

'Oh, help me!' he cried out fitfully, voicelessly. 'Help me!' And in the surrounding whirlpool of watery darkness, Josh saw the strange head again, a head with emerald eyes amidst the squall of rain, a million ripples surrounding it.

Then the rains stopped, the head disappeared and the ripples vanished.

TWO

His skin was like overripe pawpaw. He wheezed heavily, his mouth puckering like a strange bird's as he peered into the creek. He was at the far end, away from the village with its houses built on stilts, unlike any he'd seen elsewhere in the world. They were like coastland houses though they seemed very far from the ocean, and they had, too, an affinity with the forest, remote as this sometimes appeared. If one looked at them closely, their stilts sometimes lengthened, then suddenly grew shorter, slanting in the sun. It was, he reasoned, to do with the effects of the sun's sharp glare.

Pulling at his mottled beard, he looked carefully at a small toad before deciding it was a species he had already collected. But he wasn't taking any chances. He rubbed his mottled hands together for a while, then raised one hand to the side of his head, allowing it to linger on a knotted tuft of hair.

As he started walking towards the village, he saw a small group of villagers coming in his direction. He prepared himself to listen to their usual expressions of puzzlement at his activities. They stopped when they saw him.

'You see anything strange?' one of them asked when he reached them.

The stranger smiled; this was his question to them; were they parodying him? 'Just let me know what you've seen. I'll pay well.' He jingled a few coins in his pocket. 'If you see strange toads, fish, animals – whatever – I'm willing to pay.

He wiped perspiration from his arms and neck, feeling itchy and impatient in the suffocating heat. They seemed like children at times; but he suspected that they mocked him when he wasn't there.

They looked into the creek. They studied the broad-rimmed leaves floating in the stagnant water, wondering what so aroused the stranger's curiosity. They pointed amongst the weeds, but he shook his head; he was looking for something else. They watched as he continued searching, his eyes peeled like a scavenging hawk's.

From his window Josh studied the stranger. He watched him lean forward impulsively and pick up a mottled toad. Why did he look so triumphant over such an insignificant thing? Then the stranger looked up, sensing Josh's eyes on him. Josh quickly pulled his head in from the window.

But he looked out again as the stranger walked closer to the edge of the creek. A tremor went through him as he saw the man pulling at the weeds and then wading into the shallow water. He saw him pick up something that hopped like shrimp from his hands, scurrying back into the water. Josh laughed. Right then the stranger looked in his direction, their eyes meeting.

Could he tell the stranger about what he imagined under the water? No, that would be his secret: he'd tell no one about the large ripple and the mighty driftwood-like head.

The stranger picked up something else. Josh imagined him picking out everything from the creek, bit by bit, until nothing was left in it save for the old cans, shoes and bottles that the villagers threw into it. Even the alligators would be fished out and shipped far away, as he'd overheard the older villagers saying. He felt hot to the tips of his ears. This man had to go away!

His brothers and sisters, coming up beside him, noticed how he watched the stranger.

'Yuh go tu'n like he, Josh,' they teased.

'No!'

'Crazy like he!'

'You go start searchin' in the creek fo' them ugly t'ing.'

Josh kept quiet. An image of the ripples boiling like whirlpools came to him.

The others laughed louder, pointing at the stranger.

'Why you watchin' at he like madman, you eye moving roun' like marble!' one of his sisters teased.

'Me in' watchin' he!' he lied, unable to control himself.

'You are!'

'No! No!' He shook his head, as if in a fit. He wanted them to leave him alone so he could look at the placid face of the creek and regain his calm.

But they continued teasing.

'You t'ink he t'ief the creek an' tek it away, Josh?'

'Yuh t'ink he goin' mek de creek dry up?' they jeered. 'You t'ink dey gat something big-big right inside it too?'

Josh was afraid to answer. He shook with rage.

'Come na, tell we.'

'No.'

'He strange, Josh. He could wuk obeah! He could bring t'ing like massacouraman right hey!'

'Is not true!' He stared hard at them, his eyes quartz.

'He in' like we; he skin white-white an' yellow too. He in like we, brown wid the sun, an' wid mud in we skin, we eye, we ear, we voice! He in' like we – he pale like root!' When they laughed, it was as if the wind carried their laughter.

In a chorus they added, 'He like a mad man! He crazy – you gon turn like he if you don' stop looking at the creek!'

Josh closed his eyes tightly until they hurt. Tears rolled down his nose. Then the others stopped their teasing and drifted away, their laughter gone. But Josh still kept listening for it like an echo in the wind. When he didn't hear it, he opened his eyes and breathed hard with relief. He looked

17

again for the stranger. He was walking in the distance, at the point where the creek and the horizon seemed one.

'You mus' play like the rest o' them, Josh,' his mother said.

Josh lowered his head.

'Don' stay inside here jus' watchin the creek! Why you don't swim deh? You mus' learn to swim like you brother an' sister.'

Josh thought about the ripples converging on him. It'd be the same if he learnt to swim. He looked up at his mother.

'You hear me, Josh?' she pleaded, patting his arm. He wanted to tell her about the ripple, but she added, 'Or else...'

'Or else... wha'?' he whispered.

'Or else some t'ing from the creek gon pull you down, an' you won' be able to get away!'

Josh lowered his head again. 'No!' he let out in a hot whisper.

His mother walked away, shaking her head.

Josh returned to the window. This time he saw the other children swimming, as they did when the sun was hottest; saw the brown and black bodies, naked and half-naked; slim-waisted, lithe, whipping in and out of the water, hands jutting out in mock truculence or glee, in the glimmer of sun against faces, backs and buttocks. He heard the cater-wauling sounds in the splash of creek water, heard the titters; saw boy against girl, intertwining, bodies whirling about; an almost pink breast jutting out against the lip of the water; the eye of a nipple; a dark hand reaching, grabbing, fingers like tendrils in the sun, teeth flashing whitely.

Josh watched as they dove in and out, back and forth, dozens of them, talking loudly, laughing, screaming in pleasure.

Again he felt an inner frenzy.

He watched as they raced one another, as they slid down the muddy bank which became muddier and more slippery with the pressure of their naked bodies. Normally their antics amused him, but now he wanted them to leave the creek.

Close by his father said, 'You' ma tell me is time you learn to swim, Josh.'

Josh half-turned.

'You should, son.'

Josh's heart beat faster; the urgency in his father's voice alarmed him.

'Why you frighten, Josh?'

Josh kept thinking, the bathers in a blur now.

'De alligata them,' his father said, moving closer to him, 'they kyan' do you nothing.' His father's voice softened. 'Once you start splash, dey gaan. You gat to learn to swim like everybady else.' The voice hardened again.

'No!'

His father touched his arm; it felt heavy. 'Why you don' do it?'

But Josh's mind was in a delirium. He pointed to the bathers and cried, 'Tell them to go away! They disturbin' de fish!'

His father laughed. 'You mean massacouraman?'

Josh closed his eyes until his eyelids hurt, and he heard his father say, 'Come na, I go tek you by the water edge. I goin' teach you how to swim. 'Memba, the creek belong to we too, not only to de fish an alligata.'

Josh felt the strength of his father's arm against his as he was led away from the window. His legs became leaden. His father half-lifted him, then put him down again when he began moving forward. His father added, 'Don' go in, just watch the others first, eh?'

Josh screamed again, 'No! No! Leggo me!' But his voice wouldn't sound; it was trapped in his throat, riveted to his rib-cage, as he breathed hard and cried out his protest, cuffing and kicking at his father.

19

'Leave me. The creek don' belong to anybody but it!'

'It?' asked his father, taken aback, letting Josh go.

Josh didn't reply. He knew it was no use trying to tell anyone.

THREE

When the other children saw Josh, they screamed out a greeting to him, their lithe bodies rising from the water like strange fish. They ran towards him and in no time were pulling off his clothes. Josh dug his toes into the soft ground, making holes in the mud, voicelessly crying out his protest. He wished the creek would seep into the holes and totally disappear.

A couple dove in. 'See, is easy, Josh!' They splashed water noisily.

Other bathers somersaulted, totally unabashed, high-spirited, their pleasure unending. Those watching cheered loudly and looked at Josh, waiting for him to join in. But Josh was even more anxious to go back to the window and breathe calmly.

They held on to his hands and legs and brought him closer to the water. Josh smelled the creek, the rank vegetation, the rotten leaves mixed with mud. He smelled the same rank odour on the children. He felt sick, especially when they began to simulate throwing him into the creek, rocking him as if he was a hammock. He begged them to stop but they ignored him. He caught sight of his father looking puzzled about what he should do.

From his shaded spot, the stranger observed their behaviour; he did this sometimes when he was tired of looking for specimens or when the sun became overbearing and made his skin itch, made his eyes water and burn. Now the rhythm of the naked young bodies slapping against the water caused him to look with more interest, made him wish for a moment he was still young. He watched a boy, the same one who had been at the window he thought, being carried closer to the water. The stranger wiped perspiration from his neck and hands and brushed away an ant. This humidity was really too much.

There was fear in the boy's eyes, the stranger thought, sensing that this was more than a game. This galvanised him, and even though he didn't like to interfere, he got up and walked quickly towards them, stepping and skipping over the ground, something prodding him, hurling him forward.

Josh's cry was loud and clear, 'No! No! No!'

The stranger heard Josh like an echo in his own brain. 'Lemme go!'

The others laughed louder; Josh's father laughed too but uneasily. Then they saw the stranger suddenly in their midst and at once stopped and put Josh down. There was heavy silence. Josh looked at the stranger, curious, puzzled. All eyes were on the two of them, especially on the stranger, whose face was flushed red, his eyes almost livid. They'd never seen him looking like this before, he'd never really been this close to them, in the midst of their affairs.

Josh's heart beat rapidly, resounding in his arms and legs, his back and stomach. He watched the stranger being surrounded by the others. He was gesticulating, talking as if in a strange language, his mouth expanding, closing, like a fish trying to breathe on land. Josh saw his chance and slipped away, even as he heard them muttering: 'He's crazy!'

The refrain rose louder, 'He crazy bad! He mad!'

Though they were saying this of the stranger, Josh felt pained inside. He put his hands to his heart. No more beating, almost as if his heart didn't exist now.

'Mad! Mad!' the children sang, like the whir of a hundred wasps, like a rainstorm slapping the ground, the roof-tops replying, 'Mad! Mad!'

Josh turned and twisted, frantically kicking out and throwing his hands in a vain swimming motion as he felt something pulling him down to the bottom of the creek. Vast ripples surged its length. A mighty board-stiff tail swayed, creating waves that reached the houses nearest the banks, rocking them as in an earthquake. Large emerald eyes belched fire as a head surfaced. Then it plunged to the bottom before quickly tearing up through the mud and decaying vegetation. Water splashed high in the air. A gurgling sound that never seemed to end roared in his ears.

'Wake up, Josh!'

'Wha's wrong, Josh?'

'Come na, wake nuh!' sisters and brothers cried, as they surrounded him.

Josh moaned... This thing with livid eyes was still rising up and then pulling him down into the mud and slime.

'Come na, wake up! Wake up!'

Josh twitched, still moaning.

'Let we wake up Ma and Pa! Something wrong wid he!'

Josh's father and mother came and looked at him in alarm.

'Josh, is *me*, bhai!' said his father.

'Wake nuh, wake beta!' his mother wailed as she saw how twisted his face was, how he kept moaning and muttering, drops of spittle coming from his mouth.

They clustered about him, hardly giving him air to breathe.

His father looked at the others. He said, 'He dream bad.'

'Me chile sick!' his mother cried softly.

'Wake up, wake up!' they chorused again, shaking him hard as if he were the hefty limb of a guava tree.

23

This went on for half an hour. Finally, Josh was quiet, though drenched in sweat. They dabbed the wetness away from his neck and face. His mother sighed with relief, and the others sighed collectively in response.

'He gon be okay now,' she said quietly.

The others nodded.

But when they were back in their beds, they couldn't stop thinking about Josh's moaning, expecting it to start again, afraid to close their eyes. They wished for morning to come so they could get up and see that he was all right.

FOUR

Josh looked pale the next morning. His eyes were sunken, his mouth dry, lips chapped. His family looked at him expectantly; but he merely lowered his head, and when he raised it and looked directly at them, they turned away, as if unable to face him.

Throughout the day they hovered about him uneasily. His pallor disturbed them. 'Me tell yuh he come sick,' his mother said, to no one and to everyone. 'He nightmare,' she added, 'it mek he weak bad.'

Josh's father nodded reflectively.

'We have to ask he what on he mind.'

Again his father nodded, but he was thinking of the stranger, how he'd stepped in to protect Josh at the creek, and of the new boldness of the children who'd gathered around berating him.

By the evening Josh looked even paler; he had talked to no one; he wouldn't eat. His mother put fish before him. 'Is good for you,' she urged. 'Eat, Josh!'

'It mek you well,' his father said, not liking the look in the boy's eyes.

The others looked on.

'No,' Josh let out, almost voicelessly.

Father looked at mother, and frowned. They studied his face, looking at the lines caused by the dryness of his skin, his chapped, sore lips, the dullness of the eyes, and how, when he spoke, it was as if he had cork fastened in his throat.

'He have to rest,' a neighbour suggested. By now everyone had heard about Josh's nightmare; a long line of neighbours came, fussing over him.

They ushered Josh to his room and watched him quietly climb into bed. They pulled the cover over him as he closed his eyes. They left slowly with heavy hearts, muttering to one another.

But his mother could not keep away for long. To her surprise she found Josh out of bed at his usual spot at the window.

A rumour began to spread now: 'The creek do this to he, it mek he get dis sickness!'

They put their hands against his forehead to gauge his temperature, something they always did no matter what the illness. It was their pragmatic, predictable way. Once or twice his mother made a point of doing this whilst Josh was looking at the creek.

Now, no one wanted to swim there, no matter how inviting the water or how hot the sun. They gazed at it, noting the ripples and looking for strange clues. One muttered, 'De watta gat bad spirit. It catch pon he.'

When they got tired of doing this, they went to Josh urging him to speak.

'Tell we!' they pleaded.

Josh opened his mouth as if to speak, but he merely swallowed heavily and looked away, his lips quavering. They observed how his bones jutted out, how his flesh hung limp, his skin loose like a rag.

They insisted again, impatiently. 'Wha' happen las' night?'

But still Josh looked away; his lips tight, as if they were pasted together.

In their frustration, they whispered, 'Maybe is the stranger. He do somet'ing to Josh! He put bad spirit in de watta.'

Eyes rolled.

'Let we find he!'

'We go mek he say what he done to Josh!'

'T'ink how he keep lookin' for t'ing; like he gat sickness too!'

'Maybe he mad!'

'He one bad man! Look what he done to Josh!'

'We gon find he, now!'

'Where he gaan?'

'He go be at de far end of the creek lookin' fo' t'ing...'

They walked in a group to the water's edge, chattering excitedly, eyeing the tadpoles, frogs and insects with a new curiosity. One said, 'He wuk obeah wid snake an' cracadile!'

'Maybe he put it on all the t'ings in the creek. Soon it work pan all ahwe!'

'Is massacouraman he bring wid he?' one questioned nervously.

'It cyan be. Massacouraman belaang right in dis place. It na he who bring it.'

Silence, a gnawing fear; it was something they had never fully addressed before. Was it more than a myth? Real? Something that would appear before their eyes? A mighty snake, crocodile...? M-a-s-s-a-c-o-u-r-a-m-a-n? It writhed in their entrails, pain showing in their eyes.

Again they wondered about the white man. Why was he interested in such paltry things in the creek? Was he using them to put obeah on them? Some laughed to release their tension, but others growled with rising fury.

But they couldn't find him, though they looked everywhere for traces of his footsteps.

One man's eyes glinted like a new coin as an idea struck him. 'Let we look for he at night. Is then he try to catch dem t'ing.'

General approval followed and they agreed upon a time and place to meet before setting out to find the stranger. But even as they agreed, teeth bit lower lips until blood came and hearts pounded, their fear of the night hounding them.

FIVE

Night under a black sky; frogs croaking, an owl hooting lugubriously, invisible creatures hiccoughing; night's ululations and sounds they didn't recognise, which, now alert, they listened to for the first time. Unable to subdue their startled feelings, they looked at one another, drinking in each other's thoughts through the eyes. They listened, whispered to one another, and now and again nervously broke into louder talk.

Then the moon stepped out like a companion from its balcony of clouds. Now they felt more confident as they walked away from the village, along the creek. But when they turned and saw how far away they were from their houses and how close they were to the place where the silk-cotton trees grew, when they heard them swish funereally in the hurl of the wind, once more they huddled together to dispel their superstition and fear. They could hear in the wind echoes of an ancestral past of indigenous men and women fleeing into the bushes; of sugar-plantation owners, white-white, who buried slaves alive under silk-cotton trees with their own dead so their kind would be served even in the underworld; of voodoo brought from Africa to these shores; of jumbies manifesting from smelly hovels; of backoos, who worked in the sugarcane fields in the darkness of the night with an efficiency no man could match; of a plantation owner riding on a majestic white horse, dragging a heavy chain behind; of Moongazer straddling the road, head a pillar in the sky, silently watching. The wind sang too of indentured people, brown and black faces, small-framed, clutching at the *Bhagavad Gita* and reciting remnant words from the *Ramayana* in the flicker of light from the wall-lamps in narrow logies as they clung to their faith in this hostile place...

The stranger, a flashlight in his hand, was even now peering closely at the edge of the creek. They drew closer, wondering what he was doing. They saw him take out a makeshift net, unlike any they'd seen before. Each time he pulled his net up from the water he flashed his light onto it and carefully examined the contents. Now and again he took out something and put it into a bag he carried slung across his shoulders. He did this dozens of times, whistling all the while. He seemed strangely unafraid.

Then the stranger turned around as if he had heard something, flashed his light about but evidently didn't see anything. He started to head for home, but something kept him looking back. After a while he seemed to give no more thought to this and walked on.

The villagers followed, making sure he didn't see them, relieved he was still with them, that he hadn't disappeared in the darkness like a ghost.

'We gon see where he live now,' said one with increasing curiosity.

'When day come we can find he dey,' another said, as they followed him in the darkness.

The stranger entered a small, deserted-looking hut, one which they'd previously ignored.

'Dis house behind Gaad back! How he could live dey?' one asked.

'Maybe it suit he. He in' like we!'

'Yes, an' he mad too,' another added, mouth twisted in an odd jocularity and rage.

'Yes, mad! Picking out t'ings from the creek... wutliss t'ing.'

'Eh-eh, frog an' reptile... An' dead t'ing too. Maybe he wuk obeah... jus' as he done pon Josh!'

Anger rose in them, their skins feeling hotter than when the sun shone fiercely. Again thoughts of the massacouraman surfaced; was this what the stranger was searching for, this elusive thing which none of them had seen, but which appeared in their dreams, which they heard at night splashing in the creek?

One of the older ones muttered, 'Maybe he some kind of scientis'.' The word was unfamiliar to them and even the one using it didn't know exactly what it meant. The word was repeated. Then silence.

They watched the stranger close the door behind him, and waited for a dim light to appear at the window, but it didn't. They were afraid to go closer. They breathed hard, like fugitives in the night. Then, reluctantly, they started walking away, slapping the swarms of mosquitoes which they'd just become aware of. They swatted with a vengeance, swearing loudly, getting rid of their frustration, blood on their hands.

Morning came. A delegation led by Josh's father, Ghulam, headed for the stranger's hut. They walked quickly, the sunlight streaming down, bolstering their confidence. Now the stranger's power was an empty thing.

As they drew closer, though, they recalled the events of the night. Secretly they feared the stranger, silently cursing their fate for not knowing what he knew, but calling out that he must be mad to collect strange, worthless creatures that were not fit for food. Why would anyone from far want to look at these ugly things. Was their world without animals, frogs, birds, insects... without trees? Yes, he was mad; all outsiders and strangers were mad.

They stood before his door and Ghulam knocked boldly. No answer.

They knocked again. Then the door opened slowly, greeting them with the rank smell of fish and dead weeds. Some put their fingers to their nostrils. They saw the stranger's bushy head peeping out at them, like a strange animal's. His eyes were challenging and fierce. Some of the younger ones felt intimidated and withdrew a few inches.

'What do you want?' he asked.

'We wan' talk,' said Ghulam, mouth set firmly.

The stranger recognised him now. 'What about?'

'Me son... Josh –'

'Ah, the one at the window, the one you wanted to drown!' His voice was hard, intimidating.

'He have to learn how to swim,' replied Ghulam.

'Not like that. He's a child.'

'Wha' that matter? He have to learn. Me other chil'ren, dey know from early. Why not he?'

The stranger pulled at his beard and looked at Josh's father.

'Skills aren't learned like that,' he rasped.

Ghulam didn't have an immediate reply. His companions were looking around, breathing in more of the rank smell of weeds and fish and looking inquisitively at the crates and boxes in the hut in which all kinds of creatures were kept.

Then they looked at the stranger in disbelief, because this was the first time they had seen these creatures outside their natural habitat. The stranger was definitely a different kind of human being; they were convinced now of his danger.

The stranger muttered, 'They're specimens.'

'Fo' what?' one asked boldly.

'For others to study...' he tried to explain by dumb-show. 'To understand how they live...' He gave up, with a shrug.

'Wha' 'bout Josh?' Ghulam reminded.

'What about him?'

'He going to dead –'

'He can't be.'

'Is so!'

'Is he eating?' The stranger's eyes softened, showing concern.

'No.'

'Maybe he needs to see a doctor,' the stranger muttered. They frowned; there was no doctor close by. One came now and again, perhaps once every three months. Besides, a doctor cost money. Only in a grave emergency would a doctor suddenly appear, as if from nowhere, his presence another mystery.

'Maybe I will come and see him,' suggested the stranger, wheezing a little asthmatically.

They weren't expecting this. Some looked pleased, but others looked dismayed. They had expected to exact vengeance on him, but this wasn't happening.

'When?' Ghulam asked in a low tone.

'Soon.'

'How soon?' His voice rose. The others looked at him admiringly.

The stranger didn't answer immediately. Then he muttered, 'I have work to do,' and turned to his boxes. 'I will come... before he dies,' some thought they heard him say.

One or two shuddered, but the older ones, who were used to quick deaths in the village, looked at the stranger impassively.

'He cyan' die,' said the boy's father.

'I know,' replied the stranger almost gently.

'Come soon...' Ghulam pleaded.

The stranger nodded and grumbled; they weren't sure what he really said. He opened the door for them and they walked out together, like obedient children, still hearing his grunts and grumbles, as if he was chasing them away.

SIX

Alone in the hut the stranger thought about the boy. Maybe he was still suffering from the aftershock of their forcible attempts to make him swim. That wouldn't be surprising. But what if the boy had actually seen something dreadful in the creek, something that instilled an unspeakable fear in him? Maybe it was what he was looking for! He laughed to himself.

He surveyed his boxes and crates with a dissatisfied expression. He wanted something else, something that was unique, that would be the talk of Europe and America, something that would make the zoos around the world compete with one another for his specimens. This would be the crowning achievement of his career. Wasn't it for this he had come here, to live in this tropical backwater? He got up at once and started walking along the creek, towards the centre of the village. He looked at the darkness of the water, how seemingly impenetrable. He looked at the houses and thought of the people, their customs... he wished he knew more about them, about their ways, but he wasn't really an anthropologist. He saw them as simple folk without much of a history; they were people whom Sir Walter Raleigh had never met on these Guyanese shores.

But why had they come to his hut so early, so unfriendly? What was on their minds? It was something else besides the boy, some deeper fear. What had the boy really seen? Did he need to see a doctor? Could he just pine away and die? He walked faster. But when he was close to the boy's house, he stopped at the edge of the creek, at the spot he thought the boy stared at and looked steadily into the water. Bubbles... fish perhaps. A large fish maybe. No, maybe nothing at all. But he kept looking while the sun bore down on him, seeming to enter each bubble as it rose. It was nothing. Yet he crouched low, looking closer, studying the vegetation and the water lilies. Flies lightly stepped onto the water for a moment, then flew off, low – as if playing a game. But something in the water held his gaze: bubbles rising in a patch, widening. His own eyes widened, his heart beating faster.

Then he sensed someone looking at him. He looked up. It was the boy of course! Impulsively he waved.

This time the boy didn't pull in his head; instead he seemed to smile shyly.

He waved again.

The boy slowly lifted a hand, like a greeting.

He seemed well enough, the stranger thought. He pointed to the spot where the bubbles appeared, where the water seemed to boil in a frenzy.

He saw the boy getting up. A few moments later he joined him, but the bubbles now seemed to have disappeared, and the stranger wondered if his mind was playing a trick. Nevertheless he pointed to the spot. Josh looked at it without response.

'They said you were sick,' the stranger murmured, looking closely at the boy. He was indeed thin and pale.

Josh didn't say anything. He kept his eyes on the water.

'Let's walk,' suggested the stranger. Josh nodded.

They walked along the edge of the creek as the sun's rays lengthened, as shadows appeared one moment then disappeared the next. Both of them looked at the water, stopping here and there from time to time... each looking intently. But the stranger was also watching the boy to see what caught his eye.

'Did you see anything in the water?' he asked. 'Anything unusual?'

Josh took his time before answering, 'Jus' ripples.'

'Maybe you saw something... Think hard...'

Minutes passed in silence. A slow wind fanned their cheeks. The creek was softened by a mild haze as the sun burned the water.

'Eyes...'

'What eyes?'

Josh shook his head, seeming confused.

They walked on, forlorn companions, still looking at the water.

'You sure about the eyes?' the stranger muttered. Josh nodded.

'Wasn't it just a dream... a nightmare?'

Josh didn't answer. They walked further. Then Josh stopped, as if something gripped him. 'It bin dey, from one end the creek to the nex'!' He pointed a finger rigid as a rod.

The stranger couldn't make out clearly what he said, but the gist of it made him want to laugh. 'That big, Josh?'

'Yes.'

'Were you afraid?'

Josh didn't answer. He closed his eyes, shaking slightly.

'You must try hard to remember, Josh... everything!' He leant closer to the boy, coaxing. 'Is that why you're afraid of the water?'

Josh shook his head dumbly.

They continued walking. A few people turned and stared at them, alarm in their eyes. There was muttering from behind windows and doors.

'You mustn't be afraid any longer,' said the stranger, taking hold of Josh's hand despite the onlookers. Josh held onto the hand, his fingers squeezing the stranger's.

'I'll take you to my place,' the stranger added. More eyes watched. More whisperings. An hour later the stranger and

35

Josh sat before the crates in the hut at the far end of the village. Slowly and avuncularly the stranger talked about how things first came into the world: about the fish, the reptiles, the birds, the giant animals which had once lived on the earth, like the dinosaur.

Josh's eyes widened. The stranger talked about creatures like the alligators and other reptiles that were still present. Josh yawned. But the stranger kept on talking, carried away, like a schoolmaster in love with his subject.

When Josh fell asleep, the stranger continued thinking, wondering what kind of thing it could be that shook the water from one end of the creek to the other. Late into the night, he wracked his brain, opening a few books, his prized possessions (next to his specimens), reading and reflecting, mulling over one theory, then another. An odd urgency gripped him. He turned to Josh, who lay sleeping, watching his nostrils dilate as he breathed hard, as if he was remembering something.

The stranger wanted to wake him up, but he didn't. The boy was tired and underfed, though he'd seen worse in other parts of South America, in Africa and the Far East. He remembered one place in Borneo where everyone was skin and bones.

Now he wondered about his own interest in evolution. He wasn't wholly a believer in Darwinism; he had his own theories, vague though they still were, based on his observations and recorded in the drawings of various animals and birds that he'd done over the years. How carefully he'd done them, mapping out their shapes and features, tempted to see in them evidence of a vast scheme of things. Sometimes he laughed at the folly of entertaining such beliefs; at other times he was awed by his conception. He looked at the boy again.

And that one wild thought gripped him more than ever, as he patted Josh's head, feeling his forehead, which was really hot. The boy had a fever, and he pulled the blanket closer to him, fanning the mosquitoes away so he could sleep restfully. He pulled the mosquito net closer too, tucking it in more snugly at the edges. One mosquito, bigger than the others, held his attention for a while. An anopheles perhaps, and he swatted at it until its blood smeared, studying its still seething pulp.

He looked at Josh, now sleeping soundly. Then he started writing in his journal. He wrote until sleep overcame him.

SEVEN

Morning again. Soft winds, a humming as of bees somewhere, startling and yet not startling. Josh peered at the
stranger's sleepy head.

'You sleep good?' he asked.

Surprised at the question as he stirred awake, the stranger
smiled. 'Yes, Josh. How about you?' He looked carefully at
the boy, noting that the colour had returned to his face.

'What else can you remember, Josh?' He had decided not
to waste any more time. He had been thinking about which
zoo would be big enough to hold a creature the size the boy
had described. Maybe New York or London. What head-
lines there would be in the world's press!

Josh turned pale again. 'I in' know...'

'If you think hard, Josh. Maybe you'll remember something. What about the ripples? The eyes...?'

Josh shook his head as if he was dizzy.

The stranger decided he had to be patient. Maybe he'd
see this thing in the creek himself; he'd take his camera with
him next time; with luck he might get a shot of it.

He turned to Josh. There was indeed something haunted
about his eyes. But he was jumping to conclusions. Maybe
after the boy had eaten he'd be okay. He quickly put
porridge before him.

'Don't be afraid, Josh. Eat up!'

But Josh rushed to him as if he couldn't help himself.
The stranger patted the boy's soft-haired head like a father.

'You'll be alright. You must have seen something. That's what's making you react like this. It'll be over soon. Wait and see.' He wondered why he'd never married, why he'd preferred to spend his life all over the world looking for specimens. There had been no time for a wife. Suddenly his life felt empty. Only this thing, this leviathan, could fill it. Josh's face was buried against his stomach, and as he looked at his crate and boxes, he suddenly felt an instinctive revulsion for them. He breathed hard.

Josh, feeling this tremor, looked up. But the stranger merely continued patting his head. Soon after Josh started eating.

Preoccupied, the stranger walked towards the window. The sun was almost fully out. He stood there for a while until its rays hit him; the same tropical sun which he knew cracked brittle skin and flesh, especially skin like his, a man so absolutely of the temperate world. His body seemed already to be moulting. His skin had once changed in the Far East; then he'd become dark-brown, almost black – like a Negro. For a while he believed he'd contracted a strange disease. For weeks he'd itched. The villagers had laughed at him then; they'd never seen anyone who scratched as much.

Now, looking at his hands, his chest, he saw something akin to the same colour as the 'disease' and he felt uncomfortable.

Josh, following his eyes, said, 'You become like one of we,' and laughed a little.

The stranger smiled. 'Maybe,' he said, looking at his hands, pinching the skin until it hurt. He looked out at the sun, thinking of the creek and its darkish water. No he wasn't mystical or fanciful. He scowled – he was a scientist! This change of colour would be merely temporary.

'Wha' happen?' Josh asked, touching his hand. 'You don' like...' His lips seemed to tremble slightly.

39

'No – it's not that, Josh.'

'Wha' then?'

He didn't reply. He thought only that it was time they went out to the creek. He took Josh's hand. This time they walked along the opposite bank.

'Tell me what you see, Josh... anything! I must know.'

Josh didn't reply; he bent down from time to time, picking up a trifling thing and looking at it the way a boy looks at a discarded toy.

The stranger wondered if he understood Josh. 'Have you found something, Josh? What is it?'

'Nothin'.'

'Look among the weeds. Maybe you'll see something –'

'I seen everything.' Josh shuddered and turned pale.

'I'm sorry, Josh.' And the stranger, embarrassed by the boy's distress, shifted his attention back to the creek, away from him.

The villagers had also begun to take a greater interest in the creek, though everything seemed just the same. They laughed among themselves as they picked up a crustacean or a harmless reptile, then cast it back in the water. They felt that playing at being the stranger might give them some clue to his purpose.

'It na goin to be here,' one said.

'Wha' na here?'

'Massacouraman – wha' else?'

'But wha' if...?'

No answer, and they were suddenly uncertain about what they thought. It was something they had always feared in a dim, unspecific way, yet now that they thought the stranger was looking for it, they were sure that it couldn't really exist, that it was just a local legend. And then, without knowing why, they simultaneously wanted it to be real, and not to be there, afraid that it might end up in one of the stranger's crates. They wondered too about the stranger and Josh, and why Josh's father, Ghulam, didn't seem to mind.

'Maybe he could teach Josh more than we,' he tried to explain.

'What if Josh become like he? Mad like he, eh?'

'He not mad!' Ghulam answered and the argument seesawed until it lapsed into silence.

Then another asked, 'How come Josh get better wid he?'

'Eh-eh – how come?' others chorused.

Ghulam didn't know; and the question disturbed him. Josh's sisters and brothers expressed their anxieties more openly. 'Maybe he take Josh away from we.'

'No!' said Ghulam.

'He'll do it – an' Josh fo'get we!'

Josh's mother moaned.

Later that night, the frogs croaking and the insects chirping metallically, Ghulam said to his wife, 'If Josh come better wid he, maybe it good he dey. Maybe the stranger gat one special medicine he give Josh. He know t'ings we na know.' But even as he said this he was thinking about the massacouraman, and in his mind, one moment it was like a dozen camoudis all in one, and the next really small, almost invisible, something which could only be felt inside like a sudden pain.

EIGHT

'Look there,' said the stranger, alert as always.

'Wha's that?'

'That thing, like driftwood?'

The stranger had his camera ready. He took three quick shots.

'It's moving!' let out Josh, still staring ahead.

'Are you sure?' The stranger blamed his poor eyesight. 'Are you really sure?' He was becoming impatient now.

'Yes.'

Josh was staring steadily. The stranger fixed his gaze in the same direction. Then he saw it too, its eyes almost emerald in the sun.

'It's well... it's –' the stranger paused, moving up closer to the water's edge. 'It's just an alligator, boy,' he sighed.

'Alligata?' Josh's tone was excited.

The stranger took a few more shots with his camera, indulging Josh, taking a picture of him as well.

'Don' let he get away!' Josh cried. 'Kill he dead!'

'What for?'

'Kill it!' Josh was adamant.

The stranger had never seen him like this. 'It's harmless –'

'No!'

The stranger was amazed; but advancing closer to the water's edge he saw clearly a baby alligator, not more than three or four feet in length. He turned and looked at Josh whose eyes were intense, like acetylene. The stranger wasn't sure if it was the sun which caused this. Then he turned to look at the reptile, but to his relief it had gone. He forced an awkward smile and faced Josh who was still looking about excitedly.

'Ah, you won't see him now,' the stranger laughed.

'Nex' time – kill!'

'But why?'

Josh didn't answer. He was looking intently at the water, peering here and there among the weeds and pulling at the brush on the bank.

Watching his behaviour, the stranger remembered how he'd once seen a large alligator killed by one of the villagers. The stunned reptile had been dragged out of the creek and left to the youths who pulled and poked at it in the middle of the road, applauding their efforts as they dragged at the tail. A few moments later they'd lit a fire and set it against the beast. Each time the reptile twitched, they cheered, and one or two had started a chant, 'Massacouraman... massacouraman,' which had really puzzled him.

He'd been revolted by this incident and wanted to stop it, but had just gone home, exhausted by what he'd seen. That night, he'd dreamt that the other alligators crawled out of the creek and pulled the half-dead reptile back in. And the word the youths had chanted had echoed and echoed in his brain.

'But, Josh – it's a harmless alligator. It should remain where it is... in its own habitat.'

'The others, dem...' Josh blurted and then stopped.

The stranger thought he should tell Josh how important this was, now that some creatures were becoming extinct, but as he was about to speak, he was suddenly struck by the image of a great river overwhelming and swallowing everything in its wake.

Josh's voice, like a shriek, interrupted his thoughts. He looked at the boy's quivering lips... What was wrong with him?

43

'Wha' 'bout dis t'ing...?' Josh demanded. 'What you do wid he? Mas-sa-cour-a-man, eh? It really big, na?'

The stranger didn't answer. The image of being overwhelmed persisted.

Armed with a flashlight, Josh's father, Ghulam, stepped out alone into the night. He couldn't sleep and an inkling that something was about to happen haunted him. At first he had feared being out alone, but he began to get used to the darkness and his sense of expectation pushed him on.

When he had gone some distance, he looked back at his own house which, like all the others, was built on stilts because the village was below sea level. Few villagers had ever been really close to the sea, though, once in a while, when the strong north-east trade winds blew, carrying with them the pungent tang of crabs, shrimps and dead clams, everyone expressed desire to visit the seashore. At such times he too breathed in heavily and thought with a rare intensity about his own existence, about a life elsewhere, beyond the present. Then he felt at one with the elements, with the wind, the trees, the creek itself.

He walked on. Looking up he saw a faint moon, like a sick face. He looked into the water again, flashing his light left and right into the thick vegetation, into the brush on the opposite bank of the creek where there were no houses. He heard night sounds: insects, frogs, the cough of an insomniac alligator. He felt eyes looking back at him, gauging his actions. He had second thoughts about being out alone.

But he pressed on, willing himself to be at one with everything, as if his spirit could be with the insects, reptiles animals, and plants... It was then he felt himself to be most truly Hindu and yet something else. Most times he scarcely thought about his people's origins in that distant subcontinent. Here, in this isolated part of the Guyanese coastland, almost cut off from the rest of the population, they –

Indians, Africans – lived in a strange harmony, eking out a meagre living. Whatever they had been, he sensed they were becoming something else, but he couldn't sustain this thought further; such thoughts came to him suddenly, and as quickly went.

Breathing heavily, he walked on, as if invited by the night into its bosom. He flashed the light by the water's edge and stepped closer, inhaling the dankness of dead fish and rotten leaves, the rotting carcass of a snake and cow's urine. Then, a faint whiff of sea water. But dimly he sensed something else, something which had caused him to wake up and leave his wife, to walk out alone. He pictured her sleeping face, then those of his children, who often itched all night long because of the bugs in the layers of their skin, until they fell asleep, exhausted like the dead.

He saw something. He wasn't sure what it was. But warning signals passed through the whole of his body, going below the first layer of his skin and sending sudden messages to his brain. He held the light ahead of him, looking at a particular spot. He saw the commotion next. He could feel it too, as if it was inside his own bloodstream... hot, burning, rioting in his veins.

Ripples spread from one side of the creek to the other. What was it? He looked towards the centre of the commotion. He felt nausea rising in his throat. 'Oh Gaad!' he cried out soundlessly. 'Wha' happenin'?'

Suddenly the middle of the creek rose up like a great mountain, upsetting the vegetation on both banks; even the brush shook and heaved.

'Oh Gaad!' he cried again, out loud this time.

The flashlight fell from his hand, but he could still see the water lifting up, like a living being. A head next, its eyes... looking back at him! He wanted to run, but his legs seemed like tap-roots anchored deeply in the ground. Then slowly this monstrous thing submerged.

45

For an entire hour, he kept looking – dazed, afraid, unable to move, until the wind rocked him loose from the spot and he hurried home.

'Wha' wrong, man?' his wife asked, waking up as she saw him, not sure whether he'd been there beside her all the time or whether he'd actually been away.

He couldn't speak.

'Wha', man? Wha' happen?' She rubbed her eyes.

He stammered incoherently. She repeated her question, trying to take in his shaking and mumbling confusion. The children woke too, with alarm flickering in their eyes, the wall-lamp hovering like a tired, pallid moon.

NINE

Josh's father said nothing to anyone about what he had seen. His workmates were concerned by his unnaturally silent preoccupation. 'Fadda like son,' one whispered. 'True-true,' another agreed. They looked anxiously at his eyes, alarmed when they heard him talking to himself. A mumble, a mutter, then total quiet. Only his mind seemed to be at work; his eye brightening then going dull. He didn't seem like one of them any more; more like one of those from the crowded parts of the coastland, a city or town-dweller; the kind of person who, from time to time, gave way to prolonged brooding after a life of bustle and busyness; this sort – Africans, Indians or of whatever dougla mixture – were all the same, people without belief or fate, who wandered aimlessly amid the noise of jukebox and hi-fi, who swaggered drunkenly and plotted violence against each other; people who definitely didn't know hard work and thrift; who didn't know the virtue of inhaling black-sage and acacia deep in their lungs in the late afternoons when all was quiet and tranquil.

At home, Ghulam spoke little, though his wife, Savitri, persisted with her questions.

'Why you go out last night?'

'Me had to see fo' meself.'

'See wha'?'

He ignored the direct question. 'Somet'ing on me mind; somet'ing tek me outside.' She looked at his eyes, impatient with this strange, cryptic talk. She was about to scold him when, sensing this, he went and sat by the window over-looking the creek. Suddenly he felt as if he was taking Josh's place: that he had not acted wholly under his own direction.

Had Josh seen it too? He wasn't sure. He wrestled with this for a while. He thought about the whiteman; he ought to know about it. Was that why he had come there? To understand this strange thing among them? To save them from it? Could he have brought this thing with him and put it into the creek to cause havoc in their lives as an amuse-ment for himself?

He didn't go to work the next morning. He sat at home trying to recall the strange-looking face in the creek. Had it been real? When he couldn't bear thinking about it alone any longer, he set out hurriedly to find the stranger, but he wasn't in his hut. He and Josh had gone out to walk some miles further inland to where the creek narrowed, not far from where the hinterland began. Frustration pulverised Ghulam's insides. He would have to wait. He didn't want to go home, to walk alongside the creek on his way back to the centre of the village. This thing might suddenly loom up before him, taking him by surprise. As he waited he began to wonder about the creature. Was it what they called massacouraman, something which was close to him and the other villagers, which was local – wasn't from outside. Was part of himself, really. Where did such thoughts come from?

He sighed. He wished he were like the stranger, able to understand the nature of things.

Turning to walk back to the village, the stranger said to Josh, 'It's time you went home to your parents.'

Josh lowered his head; he was becoming accustomed to the stranger, his ways, his mannerisms.

'They'll be worrying about you, Josh.' He was fairly sure now Josh had imagined everything, that no leviathan really existed. Yet he still hoped Josh would talk. The boy might reveal a clue to something else. His mind wasn't fully made up, he still thought there might be something there that would finally make the world take notice of him. He smiled as he thought about this; countless scientists would want to measure it, weigh it, to discover its feeding and mating habits, its behaviour patterns – and thousands of visitors, cameras flashing, movie-cameras whirring on tripods, would flock to see it.

Josh studied the ground.

The stranger waited. There would be the book, interviews on radio and TV.

Josh shook his head, the ground swirling. 'Me wan' stay.'

'I'm flattered – I am. But you must return.'

Josh kept shaking his head, like a proud horse swishing its tail.

'This thing... it doesn't exist, does it?' the stranger said gently. Josh looked up at him, lips pursed.

'It's true, isn't it, Josh? You made it up.'

'No!'

'Ah, you've seen it then!' the stranger humoured him.

Josh looked down again; the ground swirled, like a top.

'How come nobody else has seen it?'

'Maybe –'

'Maybe what?'

'Maybe dey have.' Josh pressed his toes into the soft ground. 'Maybe dey na wan' talk –'

The stranger laughed lightly. 'Ah, Josh, they would.'

Josh shrugged, like a grownup.

And the stranger looked around, feeling like a man about to be permanently bewildered.

The rumour spread across the village, surreptitiously at first, then more openly. In each house the conversation was repeated, 'The stranger bring dis curse pon we!'

'Yuh right!'

'He one whiteman jumbieman, tekking out t'ings from the creek; an' putting t'ings in too!'

'T'ings from the land... T'ings from far.'

'Digging up the ground wid he bare hand,' they imagined. 'Now all ahwe get punish, like Josh an' he fadder!'

Ghulam, looking out from the window, heard some of these rumours, saw the alarm in people's faces, but he didn't stir.

'Dese story, dem true?' his wife asked.

He shook his head. He felt a sickness, a malaise, deep inside. And she was convinced something had taken hold of him, something she couldn't comprehend, but the same thing that had taken hold of her son. She murmured, 'We son, he life in danger. What if de white man put he into a box like animal an' t'ing?'

Ghulam didn't answer. But, when he looked into her eyes, and saw the dark pools in them, he felt as if he understood something of the terror which bemused her. He spoke slowly, with laboured breath, 'We mus' wait an' see.' Savitri scowled, her silence an arrested curse.

TEN

When the stranger heard the rumours, he was more anxious than ever that Josh return to his parents. He wondered too what had happened to Josh's father. Had he seen something too? He would have to find out. But he also began to be concerned about his security, fearing the villagers could turn hostile. He felt they were like children, swayed like the wind. What if they came to attack when he was asleep or when he was away and destroyed all his specimens?

'I'll take you back now, Josh,' he said firmly.

Josh was silent. The stranger was glad he didn't protest.

They set out for the centre of the village once more, a place which the stranger felt he was beginning to know like the back of his hand. He wanted to tell Josh this, but the latter was in no mood to listen.

'You belong to them, Josh,' the stranger coaxed, 'your parents, your brothers and sisters... your friends...'

'I in' have no friend!' Josh let out petulantly, whirring like a bee.

'You must have –'

'No!'

There was silence between them, the sun in their eyes. Clouds, vaguely grey, scudded by.

'Your mother'll be anxious to see you again. And you're well now.'

Josh's silence was like the hush when the wind falls.

The stranger added, 'You could come and see me from

time to time. I still have work to do here, though I don't know for how much longer.'

Then Josh spoke: 'This thing...'

The stranger waited until Josh broke his silence again.

'It mek bigger ripple... bigger wave... all over we village... you see!' The urgency in Josh's voice startled the stranger.

He stretched out an arm; but Josh pulled himself away.

When they reached the centre of the village, they were halted by a crowd of people with unfriendly looks on their faces, mostly the older villagers. One said to the stranger, 'You have to leave we! You wuk obeah pon we. Now go you way!'

'Yes, go away!' they clamoured.

But the stranger was not daunted. He lifted his head high, stuck out his chest boldly, hoping he could intimidate them. At once they seemed to soften, just as he had hoped. He needed time. There were the crates which would have to be taken out of the village; he'd have to wait until he made the right connections to have them trucked out.

'You wuk whiteman obeah pon we,' a woman said, almost frantic with distress. 'You go!' she pointed, demonstrating her belligerence.

But their voices cracked against his hard stare. He turned to Josh's mother. 'See, he's well.'

She nodded, looking at her son, touching his face, his hair, parting it. 'Me glad you come back.'

Josh lowered his head, digging his toes into soft ground. His mother continued 'You mus'n go way from we no more. You mus' stay with we always...'

Josh didn't respond. He glanced sideways at his brothers and sisters; then he looked at the stranger.

The stranger wondered whether there would be any point in explaining to them why they should allow him to complete his work, to give him their co-operation. He wanted to mention this new thing... What did they really know about it? He stared at each one, trying to read their minds... but he feared they were in no mood to listen.

'You mus' go!' he heard again.

'You evil... you in' like we...'

Others took up the refrain. 'Shaitan! Evil one!'

The stranger wasn't sure what to do. Their eyes had hardened beyond his comprehension. He fidgeted. His ploy hadn't worked. 'I will pay more... for specimens. I will pay you much more!' he bargained anxiously.

'No! You mus' go – now-now!'

'De evil t'ing you wuk pon we... it mek sickness,' another accused. 'Maybe somebody go dead!'

Eyes turned to Josh, who was still digging holes in the ground, as if he was digging a creek for himself.

Then to everyone's surprise, Ghulam appeared among them. 'Wait, na!' he said, just as the stranger, dismay colouring his face like an unfamiliar paint, was about to leave.

'Dis t'ing you after –' began Ghulam.

The stranger halted. 'Yes...' he muttered expectantly.

'Dis t'ing – it dey!'

The villagers were alarmed. 'Wha' t'ing?' one whispered to another. Slowly Ghulam began to describe what he'd seen.

Some persisted in disbelief, 'Is not true! Dat creek – know it good. It have nuttin' in it!'

'Wha' 'bout de massacouraman?' Ghulam rasped, eyes blinking, as if he wasn't sure about what he'd just said, but the words were said nonetheless. Then he lowered his head as he tried to blot out the image of what he had seen the previous night.

'Is not no massacouraman, is only the whiteman obeah!'

But others cried, 'It dey – it put bad-eye pon Josh an' he fadda! Them both does look out for it by de window!'

Now the whole village was drawn to the creek, startling at each sound, each ripple, each piece of driftwood or alligator's head. Any object that rose to the surface suffered death after death by gunshot wound. At night, fire burnt in their minds, raging against each board-stiff alligator's tail as it beat out the final spasms of death. A pregnant woman bawled out in her sleep, 'M-a-s-s-a-c-o-u-r-a-m-a-n!'

Each morning there was some fresh theory to pick over.

'Maybe it bad-eye de stranger firs'.'

'We have to stop he from going to the creek!'

'True, or all ahwe go dead!'

'De creek give life to we – de creek can't dead!' one lamented.

Now they were saying things they'd never said before, things they'd felt but never expressed. Fear twisted their words, trapped their feelings deep within them, though when they looked in each other's eyes, some understanding flowed. One thought of raiding the stranger's hut and setting all the creatures free. That would drive him away.

But Ghulam raised a restraining hand. 'No! Let we wait... longer...' he tried to show them he was struggling to find the words he wanted.

For a time there was a silence, like the moment of mystery at the heart of a ritual. Then Ghulam added, 'What if somet'ing dey, a big-big t'ing that eat all we fish... How we could live? He have to take it away fo we...'

No one answered. Eyes looked darkly; someone growled like a wounded hinterland creature. The pregnant woman's cry came to them once more, the utterance of the unutterable, something within themselves even as they wished it was outside them. They wanted to continue in their ordinary village lives instead of in this state of complexity. One muttered, 'Is dis t'ing really de massacouraman? We own monster in ahwe own creek. Oh Gawd!'

ELEVEN

Initial doubt gave way to complete belief. Now everyone talked about this thing that could loom up like a mountain; that could swallow whole houses; that was bigger than the biggest anaconda, crocodile, manatee and fish combined; this thing with eyes that were very small, fixed like malevolent beads in a head larger than the biggest wood-ants' nest, eyes that seemed to carry with them a knowledge of past centuries, of prehistory even... things which man couldn't understand. Compared to this thing the stranger's knowledge was miniscule, no better than that of any ordinary man. All he knew about were the tiny tadpoles or the weird reptiles no longer than a forearm or broader than a villager's foot – flat as this was through a lifetime's walking shoeless on the hard ground.

So, amidst their fear and confusion, there was also exhilaration. The object in the creek surpassed the stranger, and it was theirs. It was in their own innards, for the creek was inside them: they drank from it when the government's artesian well was dry...

They reflected on the rituals surrounding the creek: they washed and frolicked in it; they fished in it, they gained their sustenance from it. Then they imagined the thing's evil eye, erupting before them like a monstrous shadow, overwhelming all before it. It was their own insignificance they had to deal with now. They wondered what evil they'd done to deserve this.

Even in their sleep, they dreamt about it rising up like a volcano from the bowels of the creek; then, suddenly submerging, leaving in its wake millions of bubbles...

In the morning one cried out, 'We have to full-up de creek! We cyan' live like dis!'

'Full it, full it, we gat to do that!' another cried.

Tempers flared in disagreement. The older ones shook their heads in dismay; they were becoming so unlike themselves. Some went to question Ghulam, but he merely glanced at them and shook his head. His visitors marvelled at the change that had come over him – this pragmatic man who was always eager to offer solutions to their problems... They felt totally helpless.

They waited in vigil beside him, hoping vainly he would say something. They looked closely at the expression on his face, trying to decipher a message. There was nothing, only an unnatural stolidity. Once in a while Ghulam uttered a word or two, but it was as if he had a fish-bone stuck in his throat which prevented him from speaking.

His wife came up quietly beside him. She told the others to leave; he needed time to think. 'Yes, man, leave he alone, na!' Then she stood next to him, wondering about this man, the husband she'd been living with for over twenty years. And she thought, inevitably, of the thing in the creek, that it had cast an evil eye on him, on them all. She looked at Ghulam. 'Say somet'ing, man,' she urged, 'Say somet'ing.'

The stranger put down what he heard to their superstition. They weren't the kind of people given to working out solutions to difficult problems. They were too instinctive in their reactions, too fatalistic. No doubt they were even now bewailing their fears of being swallowed whole or taken to an underwater grave in the creek. He laughed to himself.

But they possessed other qualities, he reflected, lying on his stomach, sucking like an odd fish at his pipe. He thought

56

about the people he'd met in other parts of the world; there were none quite like these villagers. Breathing in, he swallowed more smoke absent-mindedly as he imagined them filling up the creek, labouring like beasts. He marvelled at their capacity for work. Pyramid-builders, Mayan-temple builders. The same plodding, the inevitable, unendurable task performed out of imagination and fear.

He lay thinking in his hammock, imagining them throwing everything they could lay their hands on into the creek: all kinds of waste cans, broken pots, pieces of board pulled from their houses with twisted nails jutting out like weapons... In a week's, a month's time, they'd stand back, fatigued, their entire bodies aching. They'd be satisfied, admiring their work, the danger gone! But then the mound they had made would remind them of a grave. Their sleeplessness would continue.

They would keep asking: Where is this thing? Is it still alive? Is it lying deep under the grave-mound waiting to rise up again in another hundred years? Then, the creek would be born once more, water seeping out of it like a spring. They would imagine the bubbles coming up... this thing showing its face to one of their children – one like Josh.

They would be sweating heavily, feeling a deep dread that they'd gone too far.

The stranger felt he'd glimpsed both the inevitability and the futility of human effort in the face of implacable nature. The urge to laughter dried in his throat as he reminded himself that he was a man with western education, with a western concept of the world. Responsibility, not laughter, was what was needed. And action, of course!

He wished Josh was still with him, for he'd gotten used to the boy. He and Josh would have talked, as much as Josh talked – at least the boy listened to everything he said. But what would he tell him? That he now believed a leviathan existed... and this was what his father had seen? Or that

Ghulam, like the other villagers, was given to superstition? That his walking out at night was a sudden bout of sleepwalking? That he, in the darkness of the night, with only a flashlight in his hand, saw what was a projection of his own fear, a shadow in his imagination?

The next night the stranger walked along the bank of the creek, flashing his light left and right as he walked towards the centre of the village. The water glistened in places, with a strange light of its own coming from somewhere at the bottom. He listened; he waited; he walked on. Ahead, he saw another light on the bank. Someone else was doing the same thing. He was curious to see what villager was bold enough to be out at night. He looked further ahead, walking slowly into the night's blackness, punctuated only by two arcs of light. Then the two arcs crisscrossed like swords, their lights flashing into the faces behind them, illuminating first their contours then their solid fullness.

'Ah – you!' said the stranger.

Ghulam blinked. 'Eh, it yuh,' he murmured, as if he didn't know how else to respond. 'Me know me gon find you!'

The stranger asked about Josh; he missed him more than he wanted to admit.

'Josh does still sit near the window, when de mood tek he. He wan' stay by heself; he always t'inking-t'inking,' Ghulam said, surprising himself by how talkative he had become.

'Is he well?'

'Eh-eh. He eat and sleep good. He de only one in we house who do. The others, dem... well... them keep fidget all night... this t'ing, you know –'

The stranger nodded; he imagined the children turning and twisting; he saw this in the other's ashen face. 'I'm sorry,' he muttered.

''Bout wha'?'

'This thing... like a plague —'

'Is not you fault.'

'I wish the others would say that.'

'Them wi' say it, once dis t'ing gone. It boun' to, nuh?'

The two men now looked at each other, their thoughts humming like the drone of invisible nightflies. The stranger had an odd feeling that Ghulam, despite what he said, despite his evident fear, didn't really want this thing to go away. For his own part, he was quite sure he wanted this creature to appear; he wanted to study it, perhaps even to capture it...

They met again the next night, each flashing his light like a signal. For a long time neither spoke. Finally, when the silence was unbearable, the stranger asked, 'So you think it will really go away?'

'It boun' to!'

'Why?'

Ghulam didn't answer. Instead he looked up at the dim moon, then at the water, where a shadow of the moon registered itself as if it were both part of the water's blackness and a reflection.

'Maybe this thing was once a small fish; maybe it has lived and grown for decades; perhaps it has grown to full size.' The stranger kept on talking while Ghulam listened and yet not listened, his thoughts wandering, going back to the far past... to Africa... This thing might have lived there in a mighty river blacker than all other rivers in the world. Had it come from there with the slaves as a curse on all the white sugar plantation owners from Europe, to lurk in the many creeks and rivers, to surge up from time to time from the depths of these dark waters? His thoughts drifted to China, then to India. Perhaps this thing had come from the Ganges, that most ancient, holy and foul of rivers, brought here by the indentured people from that land, *their* curse on the plantation owners? But what if this thing, the massacouraman, had been here since the very beginning, was native to this region, to this one spot, and had been known first by the Arawaks who prayed to it on moon-filled nights? Had they left it behind when they fled into the jungle many decades ago, as a protector of their coastland, against the likes of the whiteman or even people like themselves? His thoughts went back to his childhood; how he'd sometimes watch the creek for hours waiting for an alligator to surface. He remembered the excitement once a pair of alligator's eyes had been spotted, how he'd quickly call the others; how the news would spread, and before long the haphazard ritual of fire would begin. He sighed. The stranger looked at him but continued talking in his slow and deliberate manner.

Ghulam wondered about the stranger's background. From what he'd heard it was a place with high buildings; with doctors and nurses; with people driving fast cars and going constantly back and forth in an abnormal busyness. He imagined factories and schools, and a variety of other things to which he couldn't give a name. He wondered why the stranger didn't go back there; why he persisted in being among them.

The stranger was saying, 'Maybe you shouldn't have let the others know about it; you should've kept it to yourself.'

'Me in able to do that,' Ghulam replied with sudden sharpness.

'I would have paid you well for that secret.'

Ghulam shook his head. He was wondering about the stranger's boldness in coming amongst them and collecting things and shipping everything out. He looked directly at the stranger's face: at his jutting beard; his bold, hawklike eyes and their myriad expressions. He suddenly wondered if the stranger knew fear.

He was saying, 'Maybe if we saw this thing together, we

could do something...' He wasn't sure what. But he had imagined tying it with ropes of steel and large numbers of villagers heaving it onto the bank. He wanted to tell Josh's father this, but they walked on, not saying much, though each seemed to listen to the other's thoughts, so different in what they sought.

After an hour had passed, they separated to return home, disappointed that they hadn't seen any sign or shadow of the creature.

TWELVE

Stirrings in the water. Josh knew at once what they were. They whirred in his brain as he watched the ripples widening, as if they stemmed from a current from deep underneath. The weeds all around swirled with them.

With great effort, he pulled himself away from the window. He knew he must tell his father, but he was tongue-tied.

His father came to him. 'Wha' happen, Josh?'

But before Josh could answer, his father knew. He rushed to the window, with Josh close behind.

Finally Josh found his voice. 'Look – dey!' He pointed as the mud-brown water gurgled, as if a thousand boats were being pulled to the bottom and were trying vainly to rise up to the top again; as if the water was boiling from a source deep underneath. Ghulam rubbed his eyes. A momentary darkness overwhelmed him, in the midst of which the sky seemed to turn vermilion, like strange blood, then darkness again. He gasped, yet he tried to register every detail so he could tell the stranger.

Josh's excitement was painful; it was happening, and his father was seeing it!

'De whiteman mus' see dis at once!' said Ghulam. 'Go – tell 'e, Josh! Tell 'e now! He boun' to be in he hut.'

Josh looked at his father in alarm. He looked around, hesitating. He looked into the water, at the bubbles that seemed to look back at him. Then just when his father thought he wouldn't go, he sprinted off.

Josh ran, a bewildered look in his eyes. He passed a group standing along the main road, who looked curiously at him 'Wha' happen, Josh? Wha' you see dis time?' someone shouted as others laughed. Josh ran faster.

It was laughter which said that Josh was just a child stricken with a freak illness. As it clapped against his ears, he saw again the motley, hounding eyes in the creek.

'Tell we, Josh!' they were calling out.

'Yuh seen dis t'ing again?' the wind sang mockingly in his ears.

And they watched Josh's legs moving like a dozen legs all at once as he ran, a mere shirt in the wind, until he disappeared from sight.

The stranger was surprised to see Josh in front of him. 'What is it? Have you seen something?'

Josh heaved air into his lungs, his heart palpitating like one about to die. The stranger moved closer to him, looking anxiously at how hard he breathed, how he swallowed spittle to sate the dryness in his throat. When Josh began to froth at the corners of his mouth, the stranger was alarmed. He held Josh by the shoulders. 'What is it, Josh? Are you okay?' But looking at the boy's eyes, the stranger knew at once, just as Josh's father had known. For a moment the stranger seemed paralysed. Then with great urgency he gripped Josh and said, 'Tell me. Tell me quickly! Is it true this time? I must see it.'

Josh found his voice, though it was hardly more than a squeak, 'You gon believe?'

The stranger knew that Josh wouldn't say more. He looked about impatiently. Josh also turned, looking at the crates which suddenly seemed to him like coffins. He saw a new specimen in a far corner, something the stranger had recently acquired, a small whitish monkey; the tiniest monkey he'd ever seen. The stranger noticed Josh's interest, pointed to the monkey and laughed. The monkey jumped up and shrieked Josh's eyes brightened, but dulled again as he looked at the other animals caged in the hut. How could something as big as the creature he'd seen fit into a crate, this same thing that created the bubbles in the water as in a game; this thing suddenly thrashing about in a cage, breaking things apart, destroying itself, pieces of its arms, legs, torso, head: scattered about... Josh closed his eyes. The stranger, seeing his distress, rested a hand on his shoulder. 'You must tell me: Josh! Is it real this time? Tell me before I go...'

'No!'

'Ah,' laughed the stranger, sensing in some odd way a change in Josh's feelings, 'So you've really seen it this time?'

'No.'

The stranger grinned. 'Then I'll go an' see for myself.' He took hold of Josh's hand and, almost pulling the boy along, set off for the village.

Ghulam was waiting for them. His voice mixed excitement and disappointment. 'It gaan!' he let out. 'But it was...'

'Did you see it?' asked the stranger, still holding on Josh's arm.

'Yes... a big-big ruction... It gat to be he!' he said rapidly, his words garbled.

'Did he see it too?' the stranger asked, pointing to Josh.

'Yes, clear-clear.'

The stranger didn't seem to know what to say. He murmured to himself, 'Maybe I should wait here until it stirs again...' He sensed Josh looking hard at him. There was something going through the boy's mind that he didn't understand.

THIRTEEN

The villagers speculated obsessively. The creature had eyes as large as calabashes, teeth like spears. It had numerous appendages; it was amorphous; it defied description. Yet others claimed it was hydra-headed... With each account, something new was added. It lived far below the creek in a tunnel that wound underneath their houses. Others contradicted. It had wings like a flying horse or a bat, a flying hippopotamus and boa-constrictor combined and it flew out of the creek at night and dwelt far into the hinterland. From time to time, though, it returned to the creek. Others insisted that there was a tunnel, that it reached to the opposite side of the village, extending as far as the sea, which was where the monster came from. It was their bad luck that they had to deal with it now. Yes, the bubbles were signs of its breathing, when it was about to rise up like a mountain. Was this the creature they had called the massacouraman?

Now no one went to the creek alone. Parents forbade their children to swim in it, the women would not wash clothes there and the men no longer bathed at the water's edge after a long day in the fields. In all minds was the dread of being pulled under by the creature's cavernous mouth. Yet they needed water. Two or three would go to the creek in broad daylight, one circumspectly watching, ready to shout a warning. They dipped their pails into the creek and hurried away. Later, as their apprehension grew, they saw the very water in their pails as having the creature in it.

They refused to touch it, hardly washing, drinking, or cooking with it because they felt raw wounds in their insides, sores forming under their skins, in their armpits, between their thighs.

They walked the streets spiritless, defenceless. Only Josh's father seemed restored to his former self, though his eyes shone with an abnormal brightness. He exhorted them, 'It wi' go away!'

'How it go?'

'Same-way it come, same go.'

'How yuh know?'

'Jus' wait an' see.'

'Yuh sure?'

'Yes-yes.'

'When it gon go?'

'Soon!'

'You been talking wid de stranger!' they charged, turning to someone they could blame.

'He bring dis pon we, in one a he crate, one night when ahwe bin sleeping!'

'He put it dey, so him get de whole creek for heself!'

Ghulam, disturbed by their delirium and his own uncertainty, could only plead, 'No! Leave he alone!'

They ignored him, dismissing him as sick. They would form a delegation to confront the stranger, though for a time they didn't move, overwhelmed by their malaise. But after another night of worsening restlessness they banded together again and headed for the stranger's hut.

The stranger awoke with a start, but tired from his night walking, he fell back into a fitful sleep...

The villagers looked around the hut uneasily. They'd never been so close to the stranger before. They looked at him sleeping; he seemed so odd, almost a different form of human being. They peered inquisitively into each crate, the

66

creatures moving restlessly, aware of intruders. The villagers started back a few feet when they saw some snakes, surprised that the stranger was able to contain such creatures in his boxes.

Just then the stranger's mouth widened in a yawn, his bloodshot eyes like the sunset.

'Wake up!' they commanded, strung between their anger and fear.

'What? What are you doing here?' He looked around, dazed.

'Yuh bring dis t'ing wid yuh! Now carry it away!'

'What?'

'De t'ing in the creek dey. We see it too!'

'You have?' The stranger was fully awake now.

'Yes,' they chorused, with grim faces. 'All ahwe say dat you mus' take 'e back, put 'e into one of you crate.'

The stranger rubbed his eyes and looked at them. The ludicrousness of what they said stirred him to laughter. His tiny monkey tittered, in an odd, imitative way.

The stranger continued laughing. When he finally stopped he said, 'You must let me stay then, so I could go into the creek, under the water' – he gesticulated – 'so I could fish this thing out from the muck and grime!'

Eyes widened, as they tried to imagine this happening.

'Under de water?' one asked, his voice a squeak, appraising the stranger's nerve.

'It's the only way –' the stranger said, using his old ploy of intimidation.

'But wha' happen if...?' No one dared to spell out the consequences. What if the stranger were killed? What if he were swallowed up?

'It's mine,' the stranger said again, 'I'll take it away.' He didn't laugh this time.

It was as if they'd heard him for the first time. The impact of the words was too much for them. It galvanised their spirits with a mixture of pity and terror. One laughed loudly, another felt like weeping as he looked at the stranger, as he imagined what he'd said happening.

Then they ran out of the stranger's hut, wanting to be as far away from him as possible. Only later did they realise he had outwitted them.

Back in the village, they stood before Ghulam like lost sheep, waiting for his advice. 'Speak, Ghulam, speak,' they urged, their throats dry, their voices rasping like sandpaper rubbed against glass.

Ghulam was involved with his own thoughts, the feeling that he was changing, becoming closer to the outside world... They were all changing, though the others seemed not to be aware of this, so absorbed were they in their fear and uncertainty. But if they were changing, was it because they were being touched by all that was bad and evil in the outside world. Was this why their creek, which they had taken for granted all these years, was now suddenly alive with malevolence? Could the stranger really save them? Would he? Was he responsible for the massacouraman, pale as he was and unlike themselves? Yet, the closer they got to him, the less he seemed someone to fear.

Whilst the villagers' sandpaper voices clamoured around him, Ghulam pictured his son walking the banks of the creek with the stranger, dazzling sunlight everywhere, an image juxtaposed in his mind with his own meeting with the stranger in the dank air of the pitch-black night, two forlorn souls coming face to face in a nether world.

FOURTEEN

Now the thoughts of every household were on the stranger's promise to take the curse away. Some imagined the stranger at the bottom of the creek grappling with the serpentine body of the monster, a body harder than a dozen inflated tyres, having to use all his cunning to extricate himself.

Others realised they'd never seen the stranger with a weapon; he carried nothing except the small net in which he caught small harmless creatures. At first they laughed when they thought about this, but their laughter quickly gave way to pained distress. What if he was killed in the overwhelming blackness... with only bubbles rising up, a sure sign of death? That would mean the beast would always remain in the creek, ready to create havoc at will. None of *them* would go under... none had the skill or courage, not even Josh's father, though he went out alone at nights like a madman with his flashlight to search for this thing.

A few were hopeful that the stranger who had brought this thing would now get rid of it. He would go to the bottom of the lake in the dead of night, used as he was to the darkness, and surprise the monster. He'd come face to face with it, look directly into its beady eyes and command it to leave the creek, to crawl out and go far away, deep into the hinterland or back into the dim anonymity of the sea where it would be swallowed up and disappear forever like the giant ships that broke-up from time to time, fell to the bottom and disintegrated. Another imagined the stranger persuading the beast to retreat to its underground tunnel and remain there, dormant for another hundred years.

Josh's father mulled over the stranger's promise as he worked in the sugarcane field. He was sceptical; it was a ploy, he thought, his way of outwitting the delegation, though he didn't blame him. But he too imagined the stranger wading into the creek, turning round and waving and he, looking on, was waving back. Then the stranger was submerging, though he wasn't using a snorkel or any of the equipment that he'd heard divers wore. His mind was in a whirl; such technological details were unfamiliar abstractions. It was the confrontation of man and beast underwater that gripped him.

Suddenly he wanted to see the stranger again, to warn him about the real danger of the massacouraman. The next night he walked out with his flashlight, though more fearful than usual. There was no sign of the stranger. He was disappointed. What if the whiteman had already left the village? But Josh would know! He wouldn't leave without telling Josh.

Ghulam breathed in heavily; the creek appeared still, lifeless under the eye of the moon. He allowed his imagination to dwell on the creature, and he pictured it rising up and stretching out its tentacles like a giant octopus to pull him in. He retreated from the edge of the creek and returned home to nurse his fear.

But he continued to feel concern about the stranger's safety. The next night he set out again, keeping well away from the water's edge. This time he met the stranger.

'Dis t'ing you plan to do,' Ghulam began, 'You put yuhself in danger –'

The stranger, continuing his bluff, replied with a straight face, 'That creature's mine.'

Ghulam was taken aback; this stranger, an outsider, was claiming what, all of a sudden, he felt was part of the creek, part of the village, part of himself. His mind seesawed, because he still wasn't sure where this thing came from. He was no longer sure of anything in the darkness.

'I have to go alone; it's the only way,' the stranger said, casually swatting at a mosquito, as if what he planned to do was an ordinary, everyday task.

Ghulam was puzzled by the stranger's calm, his determination. Was it no longer a ploy? More thoughts whirled in his mind. 'Dis creek... Me swim in 'e from a boy. Me wash in 'e all me life. Me drink from 'e too-beside. Dis creek in me blood –' he stopped, as if he didn't know how to continue, rubbing his face and vaguely remembering the first day he'd learnt to swim in the creek. The memory became clearer: his eagerness to get into the water, how in less than a week he'd begun swimming. Why hadn't Josh wanted to swim? Then they heard a sound. Both men flashed their lights but it was nothing; a mere night sound, an asthmatic cough. The stranger smiled uneasily under the wordless intensity of the gaze Josh's father fixed on him.

Ghulam added quietly, 'Dey have many t'ings in the creek. Alligata, dogfish, snake, maybe a few piranha... other t'ings beside... Dey live togedder wid the –' he hesitated, not knowing how to categorise the massacouraman. It was still something indefinable, something for which he sensed the name served only as a label which was both limiting and vague. He looked directly at the stranger. The latter muttered, 'Call it what you like; they all have to live... but only for a while.'

'Wha' you mean?'

'The thing at the bottom will swallow up every thing else.' The stranger was working on the villager's fear, on his raw imagination. He noticed that Ghulam seemed to shudder.

Was it because of what he said the creature would do, or because he had hinted that it, too, was ephemeral?

In their restlessness they were constantly getting up and sitting down, seeming to take turns, one standing, looking ahead, the other sitting down until his turn came. Now both stood up together, transfixed, as if their legs had suddenly taken root. Mosquitoes buzzed around them. They slapped heavily, feeling the moistness of blood on their arms, between their fingernails. Now and again one let out an almost voiceless curse, which yet echoed far into the night. After they'd become immune to the insects, to the buzz and hum around, they again thought freely. But in their rooted fixity they no longer communicated. Only in the oneness of their imagination the monstrous head rose, as if the whole creek was rising, going upwards to the face of the moon, meeting it eye-to-eye.

They continued meeting for the next few nights, their talk filling the yawning silence. Josh's father again imagined the stranger going down under the blackness of the water, in broad daylight this time, the entire village looking on, everyone expectant as the stranger's going-down bubbles appeared, widened, grew smaller. He, like the rest of the villagers, was waiting anxiously for the stranger to return with the beast's head tucked under his arm like a trophy, then the rest of the winding, snakelike body, its skin thicker than rubber, flailing, thrashing behind. There'd be gasps and cries, like a strong wind hurling from the sea, then tremendous applause. Broad smiles next; from the stranger first; then everyone else. Then the creature would be laid out along the main road and the ritual would begin. They'd carry firebrands which they'd jab at the stunned and de-fenceless creature, which would twitch and turn in pain as it burned. The small beady eyes in the gigantic black head would roll pathetically like those of a whale in distress. The younger ones and some of the less inhibited would dance around it. This would go on all night, with sporting, drinking and laughter; young men snatching at formerly distant sweethearts who now laughed giddily; while one special young girl would offer herself to the stranger, her generosity for a deed well done. He'd refuse, of course... but only for a while. He'd look around; blush; he'd wish he was young again... That very night his blood would pulse wildly, his emotions would be free like blood from a reopened wound; he'd laugh and forget his boxes and crates. He'd be like one of them! Ghulam wanted to tell the stranger all this, but the words wouldn't come. He was about to begin when he saw the stranger's hard, determined stare. He was still looking at the creek. Suddenly it dawned on Ghulam that the stranger was determined to take this thing away. He imagined a moaning, palpitating thing, like a giant frog, being put out on display.

An intense loathing entered him and he started hurrying home, leaving the stranger alone, staring into the creek. Ghulam didn't want to think about the beast, massacouraman or whatever, any more. He wanted to be free, totally free, of all the images his imagination conjured up. He sighed a long heavy sigh, like one in mourning.

When he got in, Josh was up.

'Pa, you is alright?'

'Yes, Josh!' He breathed hard, surprised that the boy was awake. 'Why you not sleeping!'

'Me cyan' –'

'Why not?'

Josh didn't answer; he didn't know. Finally he said, 'Is he alright?'

'Who?'

'De whiteman.'

Father looked at son, wondering. He nodded.

73

'He na sick now, like dem say?'

His father shook his head once more. 'Try an' sleep,' he murmured.

Josh turned sideways on his bed, and before long he was sleeping with eyes wide-open, as his father, with closed eyes, remained awake, thinking about the stranger. This time he imagined him falling sick and leaving the aroused creature at the bottom of the creek. Then everyone's opinion would change as the rumour got around that the stranger was dying.

'Rememba how he use to mek we laugh?' someone would say. ''Memba?'

'He go dead, alone...'

'Yes-yes, he go dead!'

In Ghulam's imagination even the men lamented, and with them he heard his own voice, his own pleading. He gritted his teeth in a paroxysm of dismay and doubt. Suddenly he heard thunder like a thousand baboons howling; with his closed eyes he saw the teeth of the lightning flash in every direction. And when the eye of the storm broke, he saw in a frenzy the annihilation of everything; the creek flooding over; the beast unable to stand the onslaught of the heavy hammer-drops of rain; it crawling out from its tunnel, lying exhausted on the bank, stretched out like a long deflated tube, trying vainly to swallow the rain.

FIFTEEN

Ghulam, who was used to being out rain or shine, didn't go to the canefield the next morning. His mind festered with thoughts which seemed both alien to and rooted in his spirit. He felt as if the blood in his veins was being depleted by his heart's frenzied beating. There was no getting away from thinking about the massacouraman, how he embraced it and feared it and simultaneously denied it because he felt it wasn't truly part of himself or the villagers. Was it because they were a transplanted people? Yet he also sensed that they had begun to see themselves less and less in this light on the Guyana coastland, that somehow the landscape was changing with them, that the birds, insects, and other animals were also going through a slow transformation. Was the whiteman trying to stop that? Was that why he was putting things into crates, measuring, counting, making notes about each one? What about the inner spirit of things which was changing all the time?

He would walk for miles preoccupied with such thoughts. Once he found himself outside the stranger's hut. This time the stranger wasn't in, but Ghulam entered it absentmindedly. He surveyed the boxes and crates, which seemed to have multiplied, like living things.

When one of the animals let out a soft squeal in the gloom, he knew it was the monkey. He drew closer to it, stared eye to eye with it, noting its pupils' shiny blackness, how its face twitched like a human's as if it were about to snigger.

He looked at the pipa toad next, tried to see it with the stranger's eye. It was an odd creature, and he reflected on its oddness, and for the first time he was really struck by the oddness of things. Maybe this was what the stranger was after; his mission to let the world know this. The more Ghulam looked at the toad, the more convincing this idea became. Then his attention was caught by something scratching in a large crate, something no doubt wanting to be let out. This idea of the oddness of things left him at once.

He peered through a hole in the crate. It was an anteater, an animal which had frequently aroused his laughter because of the clumsy eagerness with which it hunted its food, as it cleared away thrash and dirt to get to the heart of an ants' nest. Once he had playfully chased after an anteater. Yet here was the stranger taking one back to his people. For what? He imagined their gazes, their surprised and amused expressions as they observed its oddness. But he was horrified too because the anteater was no longer free to roam around, to root at the heart of an ants' nest. At once he wanted to set it free. He looked around: at the toad, at the monkey – which eyed him like a watchdog.

The anteater scratched against its cage. Ghulam looked around, agitated; something burned in him, lending frenzy to his hands. He pulled at the cage door; the animal scratched even more as it sensed its freedom. Just when the animal was almost out, the stranger returned.

Ghulam stopped. He caught his breath, like a man found stealing. He bent low, crouching behind the box. He hadn't been seen yet. He watched the stranger making sure all his specimens were safe, stopping before the large box containing the anteater, muttering to himself. Ghulam felt his chest bursting. More scratching sounds. The stranger seemed satisfied all was well. Ghulam watched him light his pipe, puffing at it with wheezing satisfaction. He was very far from dying, as the rumours claimed.

Ghulam was still determined to set the creatures free, especially the anteater. He watched carefully as the stranger closed his eyes. Then he got up slowly. He looked around, he was sure the stranger would hear his heartbeat resounding in the hut, but he was breathing hard as if he was about to start snoring.

Then, just as Ghulam was about to set the anteater free, the stranger opened his eyes. The monkey let out a loud shriek, like an alarm. The stranger rubbed his eyes, as if he wasn't seeing correctly. Stupefied, Ghulam stood face-to-face before him.

'It have to go! It don't belong here!' he let out haltingly.

Surprised, the stranger growled, 'It's a specimen. It must stay here.'

The two men stared at each other uncomfortably; the stranger with disbelief, because Josh's father was the last person he expected in his hut. Quietly, but with suppressed rage, he muttered, 'They're my property!'

'Jus' like the t'ing in the creek?' Ghulam's heart beat faster; as if he wasn't in control of himself.

'Ah, that!' laughed the stranger scornfully.

Ghulam nodded inarticulately. 'Yes...' he finally let out in a loud whisper.

'I brought it here, and I'll take it with me; as I'll take all the other things.'

'Is obeah; you wuk obeah pon we.' Ghulam felt angry. He glanced at the specimens and the idea struck him that there was perhaps something odd about himself. This frightened him, not knowing if he was himself any more. He thought how different he was becoming from the rest of the villagers, just as Josh had been from the beginning. Then in a moment of blind insight he cried out, 'If you let dese t'ings go, maybe that go too.'

This 'logic' caused the stranger to raise his eyebrows. His gaze slowly shifted to the anteater, to the monkey, to the pipa toad, to the reptiles and other things in his crates and boxes. He smiled. The boy's father couldn't stand the silence; he watched as the stranger's forehead seemed to expand and shrink into furrows. Suddenly the stranger said, as if with great deliberation, 'It's a dead thing in the creek –'

'Dead?'

'Yes.'

'How you know?'

The stranger seemed to grin, even though the furrows remained in his forehead. 'I'm not mistaken,' he murmured.

Ghulam felt more confused. Was the stranger telling him the truth? A sense of his gullibility irked him; could he trust what he'd seen... the bubbles, the commotion in the middle of the creek... He was angry with the stranger's ploys. His tongue cleaved to the roof of his mouth. He saw the thing in the creek floating, like a huge cow, bloated, with a thousand dogfish all around it jabbing at it with their sharp teeth, raising a stink that would remain in everyone's nostrils for years to come.

Once more the anteater scratched in its box. Ghulam looked from the crate to the stranger. Something had separated them, something which he didn't know much about. He drifted out of the hut, images of the dead, lifeless thing in the creek, swelling, creating havoc in his imagination. Outside he knew he wanted the creature to be alive. The feeling made him quiver like a man demented. He clutched at his throat as if he felt an intense pain there. And fleetingly he imagined the anteater still locked in its cage – himself in the cage. When he reached the village he was soon surrounded by questioning voices. They sensed he'd come from the stranger's hut. What was he doing? They looked anxiously as Ghulam appeared to convulse, his eyes rolling.

'What happen dey?' they demanded.

'Tell we, Ghulam.'

'The thing...' he let out – 'He say it dead!'

'Dead?'

'Yes,' he laughed, without any obvious connection.

The others at once also began laughing; and in the midst of their laughter, his longing grew that this thing in the creek should be alive. He wanted those who came from outside, those from far, to see that this thing was theirs; that it stemmed from them and in a way defined them; massacouraman or whatever name it was known by; that it was part of their identity on this Guyana coastland; part of what made them appear odd but recognisable.

SIXTEEN

From whence things came and whither they shall return; the phrases echoed in the stranger's mind as he lay in his hammock. What of that final melding with earth, water, fire and air? What sense was he making when he thought about the insistent smell of things and the infinite spirit of objects – organic and inorganic? It was all metaphysics! And he was a scientist. It wasn't for him to think about the spirit of things. Yet as he looked at the range of expressions on the monkey's face, he saw himself as in a mirror. He laughed. The monkey laughed too. He moved closer and looked into the shiny blackness of the creature's eyes and he was sure there was a quality of life which was present in all things. He checked himself; he was a man given to empirical investigation; to the study of habitats, measured, documented, recorded in a journal at regular intervals. He didn't try to wrestle with the deeper meanings of objects, with the value of existence. Such metaphysical and philosophical excursions were of no value to him. But a question hummed in his mind, despite himself. If environments shaped objects, why not the opposite?

But like an ingrained habit, he returned to the immediacy of his specimens, to the monkey's facial twitches so like his own; to the rush of the anteater in its cage – so like the villagers' hurried departure. His mind hummed with such correspondences. He felt troubled because he had always wanted things defined, pigeon-holed, classified.

What was happening to him? He reminded himself that the expedition had really been quite successful; he'd managed to collect many new specimens and now, perhaps, the big triumph of his life was imminent. He sank deeper into his hammock, his imagination dipping and turning as in a dream. He was there with Sir Walter Raleigh, with his son and Lawrence Keymis on their coming to these shores. What had the indigenous people thought when they had first seen a white man? What had they felt when they encountered the stern gaze of these Englishmen who had hacked a trail through the mighty tangle of green thickets, asking if the city of El Dorado really existed? Could he see himself as a descendant of Raleigh? At least he followed in his footsteps, though perhaps he was more akin to Darwin; maybe he combined them both in his relentless search for new species, new traces of evolution... And what of these people here, the villagers? He knew where they had migrated from, but what were they now? What were they becoming?

Later that night, unable to rest any more, he walked out; he'd become truly nocturnal so he could walk by the creek, without disturbance from the villagers.

Now it wasn't so late, merely darkening, with the sun going down, a wash of colours in the sky. He marvelled at the tropical sunset – it was like nothing else in the world. The clouds were like multicoloured blinds, shapes and shadows, burgeoning, disappearing. The stranger looked up. The more he looked at the shapes and shadows, at the russet, vermilion, the ochre, everything with a marvellous restlessness, the more he sensed a giant melding taking place... Again he felt he was being detached from his usual self, rational, pragmatic. But who was he? Raleigh, Darwin or some other forerunner unknown? Whose spectre would he eventually take on? It was as if his mind was becoming separated from him. He'd only felt this way once before, in

Borneo, where he'd suffered a severe bout of malaria. In the midst of his fever he'd cried out, 'O God, please save me!' and felt embarrassed when he was told about it later. All he remembered was feeling vague, feeling unlike himself.

Again he looked at the vermilion in the sky. A wide wash of it, like a blaze, a Biblical burning bush in the sky. Fancifully he imagined the bearded Moses of his childhood picture books being catapulted up to it! He felt himself being pulled up too, slowly, like walking up a mountain without effort. He rubbed his eyes. He was an object in a painting, walking on air, insubstantial, but moving, defying gravity, space and time. Then, like an Icarus, he began coming down, his wings falling off, blown away – like the loss of one's trousers. And he paddled with his feet in watery space like some floundering misplaced fish, before he landed firmly with the awkwardness of an earthbound ape in a tree, its branches leaning low...

Rubbing his eyes, relieved that he was still on the ground, he walked on, away from the outskirts of the village, following the winding creek. As it darkened, as the moon began to appear; the colours faded. What began as a vague feeling of dismay became a sickening emptiness. He longed for something to fill this void, but he felt instead a tearing inside him, making him feel like a shadowless object, without body or substance.

He was desperate to separate what was real from what wasn't. His eyes searched the creek; the sheer blackness of it. There was something which was either a large head or the substanceless image of something in his mind. As if against his will, he stopped, moving closer to the water's edge, and he was only himself now, no one else, looking at what was before him, as in a mirror. There were eyes, like those of an old man, with corrugated skin around them, webby eyelids like flaps. His heart beat faster; he looked carefully. He studied what ought to have been a mouth, but was merely a crevice. A nose, the contours of a face. It wasn't just his imagination he kept telling himself; or a vagrant moon's ray, or a remnant shadow from the sun.

He saw the outlines of an entire body; a huge protuberant stomach like a giant black tube, floating. An extended torso next, a back, and a tail wagging lazily, creating bubbles all around it.

He realised how close he was to it. He looked up at the moon. Did this image exist only in his head? How could he measure or classify what was before him? Again he breathed hard, like a man in a hurry, who had to leave, yet who felt forced to remain longer. He looked at the apertures, at the eyes in particular, and felt himself drawn towards it. He felt needles tingle his spine, then spread to every part of his body. Despite his shock, he kept his eyes fixed on the creature's huge tail. He felt like a split person – one part of himself elsewhere, still with the clouds, aloof and immune, while the other part was firmly on the ground experiencing this enormity. Yet both selves seemed one in an awareness of this thing, in its terrible beauty.

The eyes looked back at him, still seemingly ferocious in intent, the head looming up above the water, the body distending, heaving, like a huge boulder, the water falling off on both sides, the tail moving back and forth in synchronised motion with the rest of the body.

He felt himself drawn into the water, the motion of the tail causing waves to flap against his legs. It was only when he nearly stumbled that a concern for his safety returned. Grabbing hold of the vegetation near him, he tried to pull himself out, but felt as if the bank was being pulled from under his feet. He grasped desperately at an overhanging bush as more water quaked against his legs. He knew now this wasn't a mere imaginary fancy. The eyes, carrying a luminous moon in them, glared at him. For an infinitesimal moment, the thought of death as a tempting new journey flashed into his mind, but the instinct to survive, ingrained in him from early, forced him to struggle, to hold on. He pulled himself out this time, with sudden gladness, before he could be pulled down into the miry depths of the creek. It had been mere bravado when he'd said he'd do this of his own accord. His heart beat with hammer-blows; his entire body was hot and heavy, a palpable shadow closing in, overwhelming him. He wasn't sure how long this feeling lasted. Then the heaviness seemed to disappear. He turned. Faced it. A mere reflection... then not a reflection. Nothing! He rubbed his eyes in disbelief.

The need to hold on to some objective facts seared him. He looked around, bewildered. Those whom he passed on the way through the village looked at him with shock, at his clothes splattered with mud. His eyes were no longer intimidating; he seemed dazed, forlorn, distant. Some illness was taking its toll on him. He didn't respond when they greeted him with curious pity; he just stared dully ahead not registering what they were saying.

'Is really he?'

'Wid mud all over he clothes! He change!'

'He bin to the creek... alone!'

'Tha's not possible... the t'ing –'

'Maybe he fight wid it and it do this to he –'

'He kill it?'

'Yes-yes.'

'Na, man, he na able to dat!'

'Maybe dat t'ing dead – people di' say he gon kill it!'

Opinions seesawed as they watched him walk on; as he reached the familiar spot under the window. They saw him looking up. Josh was there. He waved, because he knew at once. The stranger didn't wave back but turned and looked towards the original spot where the boy had first seen the bubbles. Was it possible that things from prehistory still lived? His mind felt addled at this evidence of the concreteness, yet mystery of objects; his divided selves spoke to him like twin messengers with contrary tales.

'Is me – wait fo' me!' Josh shouted, running down the stairs with a new-found spirit. 'Whe' you goin'?'

The stranger didn't reply; he walked on like a drunken man.

'Is me – Josh! Hear me! Now you mus' tell me!'

The stranger stopped, turned around, but only for a second, as if he was making sure it was Josh. Then he continued walking.

'De t'ing in the creek... It na real!' Josh cried out. It was as if he was speaking with the voice of his father; his mother; his brothers and sisters; with the voice of the entire village. The stranger scowled; his eyes hardening like marbles.

Josh suddenly laughed – irrepressibly. Bewildered, the stranger walked on, like a man in a hurry to be nowhere.

SEVENTEEN

To the children the stranger had never seemed more odd. He seemed to be carrying some terrible burden as he headed for the deep hinterland away from the village. They followed him, laughing and jeering, led by Josh whose new-found spirit put him at their head.

The stranger, his mind in a swirl, recalled the currents in the water, the face he had seen, the eyes. The futility of his life dawned on him – an empty life spent collecting speci-mens. Why? Why not let things remain the way they were, retaining their mystery, their malevolence too, all through the centuries? He walked faster; the laughter of the children like a flock of parrots mocking in his ears. He walked on, fury in his veins, stepping faster, yearning for respite. And the jeering of the children, like Eumenides, deepened the conflict in his mind.

Josh's voice taunted, 'Is a dead thing you see?'

Others: 'Dead-dead-dead!'

'No!' he let out voicelessly.

'You dead too!'

'Yes – you is a dead man walking! You been sick – you a jumbie now!'

The voices clapped against his ears like the rustle of leaves from a thousand trees, like old boards cracking in intense heat, like the first drops of rain protesting their fall from the clouds. They were at first shrill, then frenzied like fire sweeping sugarcane fields. He walked faster as the voices jabbed at him. But he felt a dazed immunity from their assaults. He despised what he stood for; despised categorising the objects in his boxes and crates. Now he wanted all his specimens to be free, creatures roaming wildly, like the children.

Fleetingly a Pied Piper feeling took hold of him. He imagined going to the sea where a large ship waited. Embarking with the children, he was the master mariner, setting sail for a horizon curved like the hump of a whale's back. He'd go to the point where he saw the bone of sky, the flesh of clouds, the blood in the rainbow, where everything throbbed like a giant heart. But in the tremor of his nerves he imagined the ship being followed by the creature which had crawled out from the creek. When it loomed up from the bowels of the sea, the children applauded!

The adults were amazed at the excitement in the village, its resuscitation and revival. They watched this new alertness through jalousies and windows, hearing the children's shrill voices, faces stretched like rubber in gladness.

Savitri said to her husband, 'Maybe he leave we soon.'

'He gon stay,' he replied.

'Why?'

'Dat t'ing, he see it! It keep he here! He come one o' we now – fo' good!'

'One of we?'

'Yes-yes – dat t'ing, it gon haunt he like it haunt the rest o' we...'

'But de t'ing dead!'

He shrugged noncommitally and she glanced sharply at him, puzzled about what he meant. She didn't press him, but as she watched the stranger in the distance, with dozens of children following him, something odd about life struck a whirring blow in her brain. She closed her eyes slowly, as if in pain.

There were other villagers watching the stranger who was turning around to face the children, waving his arms like windmills, flailing at them, defending himself. They could see the tension in his face, the deepening grooves of each grimace caught by the angle of the sun. He walked about in a circle, as if in an odd dance, the children all around him, shouting their triumphant chorus. From the distance, caught in the sun's brilliance, the children and the stranger seemed one.

A few emerged from their hiding places, not sure what to do. 'Maybe de chil'ren should leave he now,' one said.

'It serve he good!' another replied; but without conviction. One woman first, then half a dozen others quickly stepped forward, as if propelled by a maternal desire to protect.

'Leave he alone!'

'Yes – leave he in peace.'

The replies came like hollow sounds reverberating in a tunnel.

'He dead – he dead!'

'Is true – ask Josh!'

Josh's voice, 'Ask he to speak... see... He won'! He see de dead t'ing in the creek... It mek he dead too! Same-same! Like massacouraman!'

'Did 'e kill de t'ing?' another asked, bewildered.

No answer; just shrill incomprehension, then silence.

Had his dream been the result of malaria, the stranger wondered. Or yellow fever. His joints ached and his bones felt stripped of flesh. Was this one of those terrible wasting tropical diseases? He couldn't think clearly... he needed help! He wished he was back in a place of civilisation where there were hospitals, a doctor, a telephone so he could call someone... an emergency! He bent forward, crouching, getting up, still thinking about his dream. Had he been dead? Voices rustled in his ears like beetles. His mind drifted: he was back as a choirboy singing in church; biblical Joseph and his dream. Was he dying, or had he already died and been born again? Yet as he looked at his boxes and crates, he thought immediately of all the work he had to do. A journal to write, articles to prepare for scholarly publications, lectures to give. Commitments to zoos and museums. But did it mean anything any more? He retched; a deep sickness in his stomach.

EIGHTEEN

Josh felt an immediate freshness as he entered the water. There was nothing else to be conscious of, no self-consciousness about the others watching him. He felt as if he had been used to the water all his life. There was no pressure as the water's blackness surrounded him, as it swirled, as it engulfed him. It was like being swallowed; he laughed, enjoying the sensation, the warmth. Saliva-warm. Josh could feel the sun in the water, creating new life. Josh didn't look at his friends, but their applause drifted like soft rain to his ears. He stretched out his legs and arms as he'd seen others do. He paddled, waded, paddled. Swam, almost. Once he turned and looked back at them, their smiles, their laughter, their inevitable words of advice. But nothing really registered except being in the water. He floated. He was a log. He felt both overwhelmed and borne up by the creek. It claimed him, but it was all his now.

Becoming bolder, he floated further, almost to the middle. Amazed at himself, at how easily he moved, he floated on, propelled, it seemed, by the wind.

His mother said, 'Why he na wan' swim befo'?'

Ghulam didn't answer.

She added, 'See how good he swim!'

'Yes.'

'He kick out strong, jus' like the rest.'

'Yes, he could be –'

90

'Born wid it!' She looked at him, then shifted her gaze once more to the celebration of water rising up in the air, being held in suspense there like a miracle, before crashing down like a waterfall. Some of the adults were joining in now; they didn't do this often, such cavorting was for their younger days. But they felt inspired by Josh; they couldn't help themselves. And the water no longer appeared black; its opacity gave way to a crystalline clarity. They saw themselves through it; they looked at each other while they were underneath it; they surfaced, with their eyes and mouths brimful with water, and they still saw clearly. They called out to each other. Adults lifted children on their shoulders and flung them through the air, shrieking with excitement as they fell, like brown unfolding rocks. Laughter. The water warm like spittle, like clay dug fresh from the ground after the softening of tropical rain.

The stranger walked on water. Yet his lips were parched, his skin hot. He was thirstier than he'd ever felt before. He badly wanted to drink, but when he bent down to scoop up water in his hands, as he'd seen the villagers do, when he brought them to his mouth, they were always empty. He wanted dates and grapes, hanging things he could reach out for with his hands, to feel their softness, like a woman's breasts, against his mouth. He ached for a cool spring percolating among stones and boulders. Suddenly he began to sink, like a holed, rudderless ship. He floundered, going down, Lazarus, to an ancient grave. He was half-buried in solid ground next, unable to sink any further. Vultures hovered, coming closer to have a good look at him, with horny faces, leprous-looking bills. They landed, pecking at each other as they vied for him, to pluck chunks of flesh from his neck, his face, where the skin peeled and dripped, like ice melting in the fierce heat of the sun.

He felt weaker. The plucking began, the sensation dizzying him. Each jab, a jolt in his head. Each a hammer-blow. He became bone before his own eyes. The victorious vulture's eyes, like incandescent balls, came closer. He saw Josh's eyes. Josh staring at him!

Startled, he woke up. Light streamed through his hut. The monkey's loud chatter greeted his ears. He wasn't sure how long he'd been there, how long he'd been ill. But something gnawed at the pit of his stomach. A fierce hunger. Perhaps his illness was over. The increasing hunger goaded like a raw wound. It was a sign of health, of the body's need, he told himself. But at once he remembered the vulture. He closed his eyes. Then opened them again. The monkey made a face at him. Maybe he'd been sick for the whole of the past week.

He ate hungrily the remaining biscuits and mouldy cheese. Each time he swallowed he felt hungrier, but a little strength returned to his body as well. He began to see better now. And stretching out his arms and legs, he felt a great tightness had gone from him. He got up and walked out of the darkness of the hut, out of the dank air, into the fresh brightness of the sun. He inhaled fresh grass which crinkled his nostrils. He walked a few yards more, filling his lungs to capacity. How good the aromas, the wayside zinnias and lilies, the jasmines strong in his nostrils. He gathered a few flowers and unconsciously made a bouquet as he walked along, the red hibiscus festooned about him.

He walked lightly, as if he was walking on air. He couldn't feel his heart beating; everything was effortless. Now he wasn't sure if he was still dreaming or not. But he didn't care; his euphoria sustained itself the further he walked. He felt his hair rich and thick, his skin smooth as if he was still a youth. He looked around. The houses seemed to have taken root in the ground like trees. He walked around them in silence. No one was about. Where were they?

Then an image of the leviathan arrested him, tightened

round his throat. It felt so real he put his hands to his neck. He began to walk faster, his heart beating against his ribs. He wanted to see Josh, overcome by a great anxiety for the boy's safety and by the memory of the vulture's eyes.

He seemed to walk endlessly before he reached the house with the familiar window. He looked up. Josh wasn't there. The thought came to him that now was the time to leave the village. Most of his work was done, but then he remembered he couldn't take out his boxes and crates without the villagers' help; he felt trapped.

Where was everyone?

The deadness of the village weighed heavily on him and he felt pummelled inside. Had he lost control of his senses? Had he been poisoned by the leftover food he'd eaten? He wondered if the villagers had locked themselves in their houses when they saw him coming. But this was not like them, always peeping out from somewhere, such was the curiosity he aroused in them. He remembered the children's laughter; the parents' fear. He turned, slowly; he would have to face the creek. He remembered how much they'd wanted to fill it up, a grave for the leviathan. What if the creature had risen up and swallowed each one of them? In his mind's eye the water was deathly still, but he imagined an immense swallowing had taken place. Josh had been the first to disappear; screaming, looking back only once, arms and legs flailing, crying out for help! All this had happened while he'd been sick. He felt like a Rip van Winkle waking up into an empty world.

Was it his turn now?

He imagined himself being swallowed; his body, emaciated but wiry, was being pulled in; that same face, mysterious, malevolent, was drawing him in against his will. Froth oozed all over him, the way he'd once seen an anaconda do as it started swallowing a pig, and he imagined a slimy throat, like a tunnel, from which there was no escape. He saw foul-smelling things pasted there as he fell. Into the tangle of stomach, a quagmire of blood vessels, mud, garbage and half-mangled human bodies. He squirmed, fought to get out. 'Oh God!' he cried.

At once he began hurrying back to his hut, like a man demented, as if the leviathan was running like a leopard behind him. But he had an odd sense that he was being chased by himself.

Faster!

Inside his hut, he breathed a sigh of relief. Then, panting heavily, he took stock, like a man who had woken from sleepwalking, but was still unsure of himself, disoriented by the nightmare and the simultaneous reality of the life he lived.

NINETEEN

Josh flailed arms and legs in the struggle of the true swimmer he was becoming. He heaved in more air; he felt like a flying fish as he felt his body lifted above the water for a moment. The opposite bank came closer, as if drawn by a magnet in his eyes. 'Swim, Josh! Hol' on now!' he heard his brother call, though his ears sang with dizziness. For a moment he felt he was being pulled under, but more shouts of encouragement slapped against his ears. His muscles ached, as a hand reached out to him, then others all around him. 'Go, Josh! Hol' it, bhai! You deh now! You reach!' But his ears sang and, for a while, he felt he was being sucked down into the murk and mire.

Water swirled in eddies around him. He was alone in an ocean, huge waves rising, spray flying as sudden currents clashed. Though he felt their hands, it was as if *he* no longer existed; he was mere floating weed and cork, and the others around him were floating objects too. In his dizziness he saw the entire village floundering, the houses breaking up like small boats; boards and beams scattered everywhere like matchsticks.

'Keep yuh hold, Josh! Hold de grass an' mud! You gon do it!' He felt they were playing a game with him, laughing and tormenting him, goading him on, yet trying to prevent him from succeeding in this final moment. Just then he thought he heard a soft cry – 'Massacouraman!' Was it his father's voice? Was it the stranger's? He couldn't tell, only that the word came to him again in the wind's siren voice.

He gripped the bank before him; his eyes closed. Voices, like the wind echoing in conch-shells on a faraway beach, buffeted his ears. He wasn't sure what happened next. He was stretching out an arm; he was a fish, scaly all over, the same fish he'd watched so many times from the window. He remembered the bubbles, each sucking him in. His senses were confused. It was dream, oblivion, a Oneness. He couldn't tell. Exhausted, he sat on the bank, head lowered, breathing heavily. He looked above the heads of the other children and at that moment he realised that, more than anything, he wanted the stranger to have seen what he had done. He saw his father and mother, both waving. He listened to the clapping hands. He felt mud and bits of grass between his legs, his buttocks. He tingled all over, sitting deaf amidst the clamour.

'Josh, wha' happen?'

'Why yuh don' speak, Josh?'

His skin burned in the sun, his eyes blurred. Though the others pressed, he remained silent. 'Mass-a-cour-a-man,' he whispered to himself.

'You have to swim back now, Josh. Yuh ready?'

The clamouring stopped when they realised Josh wasn't hearing them, but their eyes continued to question.

He resisted, looking at their frowning faces, as if he didn't know them, even his brothers and sisters. Suddenly he gasped, 'De stranger, where he gaan?' his tongue, heavy, his ears a whirring chaos.

It was as if the others didn't know what he was talking about, had forgotten the stranger. Yet from the determined look in Josh's eyes, they at once reconstructed an image of the whiteman, like an illness in their midst.

Josh's father appeared now on the opposite bank. He hallooed across to Josh, 'De stranger gaan! He leave we! He gaan, Josh!'

No one stirred; the sound reverberated.

Father looked at son across the creek. 'He dead... gaan!' repeated Ghulam, his expression rigid, his voice suggesting both anguish and joy.

The others let this sink in for a while.

'Gaan? He really gaan?' they repeated, as if they had developed some strange form of madness. Only Josh, looking steadily into the water, shook his head, disbelieving. He looked for his reflection, but the mirror surface was broken by his dangling feet.

Skeletons of snakes hanging from the rafters like strange decorations; stuffed reptiles gathering an embroidery of cobwebs; a crocodile's cavernous jaw with its teeth jutting out like short, sharp spears; a stuffed bird trapped timelessly in motion: these taxidermic images settled in Josh's mind like a foul dust as he headed towards the stranger's hut.

To his amazement when he reached there, the hut seemed the same as ever. But he saw, to his surprise, that the boxes and crates were empty, save for a few sickly-looking animals in one or two of them. The smell of rotting vegetation had gone.

Josh breathed hard as he looked around uneasily. He went closer to the boxes, almost expecting the creatures to materialise. Had the stranger let them out himself? One by one... the anteater, the monkey, the baby alligators; even the pipa toad which he cherished?

The stranger... where was he now?

Then Josh saw him in a corner, rolled up like a bundle. For a moment Josh feared he was dead, but the stranger's rib cage was rising and falling. He was thinner; his eyelids seemed ribbed, horned, fluttering like sensing devices. He seemed so much older, but lay in an innocent posture like a child. Josh looked at the rest of the body, insignificant as driftwood.

An arm stirred. Then a leg. Then both together. The right arm moved to the face, to the eyes. Rubbing. Then the eyes opened and closed in an instant. They opened again, blurry; unable to focus.

'Josh!' whispered the stranger. The entire shroud stirred.

Josh waited, his heart pounding.

'You! How long have you been here?' he asked, trying to get up.

Josh moved a few inches closer. 'You... di' dead!'

'What? Dead?' The stranger moaned softly. He looked dismayed, as if what he was seeing was still part of his dream. He felt his joints squeak like rusted hinges. At last, slowly, he managed to pull himself halfway up. Josh smiled, 'You alive now!'

'Yes – I am!'

'You di' dead –'

'Why d'you say that?'

Josh didn't answer. The smile disappeared. He turned, looking at the crates and boxes. He pointed. The stranger rubbed his eyes in disbelief.

'It can't be – they're all gone!' He grimaced in dismay. Josh, seeing this expression, immediately laughed. But the stranger added with despair, 'All my work – it's all gone!'

'It have mo' deh.'

'You don't understand!' the stranger insisted, confused, dizzy. 'I guess I've been dreaming a lot, I was sure *you* were all gone! Not my specimens.'

Josh studied the stranger's chin, the thick beard; how the eyes seemed to be ablaze one moment, then dull another. They were dim now.

'Me came see if you really dead,' Josh said slowly as the eyes dulled even more.

The stranger decided to humour him a little. 'What else?'

Josh didn't know what to say. Then he let out, his eyes alight, 'I able to swim now! Me di' want you to see!' The stranger smiled as he thought of the boy's earlier fear of the creek.

'I'm glad you can now.'

But Josh was eager to say more. 'I can swim dey an' back. You have to see me!'

The stranger nodded, amazed at the boy's mounting excitement, a foil to his own dismay. As Josh continued animatedly, the stranger wondered about the loss of his work. The boy's rain of words brought home to him again the sense of futility he'd felt before; his feelings of sickness and mortality. Yet he also felt that the halves of himself were now becoming one. He tried to imagine the boy swimming across the creek, and he wished he was someone who could paint or draw, who could create out of the bottomless pool of his mind some image of what he was thinking now. And his mind, inevitably, went back to the leviathan, this thing they called the massacouraman, which had dominated the creek for so long in the solitary eye of the imagination; which was palpably flesh as well as spirit. How he festered, like an old disease.

TWENTY

The chocolate-coloured water was placid. There were the usual bubbles; the floating vegetation; weeds; the fish causing ripples; a loud splash somewhere. The village was astir with voices; laughter; a child's boisterous cry followed a few seconds later by a mother's cuddling sounds; Josh's brothers and sisters running excitedly in and out of the doors of the house; dogs barking; an old man's mocking, crotchety cursing.

'Everyt'ing de same – jus' like when you come,' Josh said to the stranger.

The stranger nodded; he walked along, trying to remember what it had been like, but his memories were not strong or persistent. Something else had taken over his mind: the feeling that he was now someone else, that he had become like one of the villagers.

The villagers nodded to him in greeting. The stranger responded politely. There were smiles, an easy familiarity. They stopped and talked, called him by his indistinguishable surname. The stranger was no longer a stranger, in mood or spirit. His skin, at first mottled, was now healthily dark. His hard-edged pragmatism had given way to a mild openness. He no longer walked along the edge of the creek picking up objects. His odd behaviour was over, though some of the villagers wondered if he was still mad, if he'd really become different as a result of his illness. Others countered, 'He just like all ahwe now. He act like we, not so?' Yet a few always recalled the reason for his presence among them. They still saw him as an outsider – he'd always be that. Perhaps only Josh thought differently. Some thought it good to have him among them: it was the only way for the village to be in contact with the outside world, though one said loudly, 'He come from outside; he bring evil t'ing wid he.' But others laughed dismissively, thinking this was meant merely as humour.

As for the stranger, he drifted along in a kind of insubstantiality, as if he had accepted the creek's mildness in himself, was one with the flow, the ripples, the fish, the weeds.

Josh's father said to Savitri, 'It funny how he and Josh get along so good. It like he Josh second fadder.' He laughed and she laughed too, though she speculated privately about the possibility of the stranger marrying one of them, and then perhaps having a son of his own. But she dismissed this thought; he didn't seem the marrying kind.

Once, indeed, Josh told the stranger that he should come and live with them. But the stranger was hesitant, he talked vaguely about independence, but it seemed as if he wasn't sure what he wanted. Josh laughed, 'Eh-eh, you still de same?' The stranger smiled.

Now they never talked about the thing in the creek; it was taboo. They merely looked at the creek from time to time and admired the pattern and symmetry of the ripples. But one morning Josh felt agitated as they walked beside it. He'd had a sleepless night, the result of an earlier taunting from his brothers, and during his wakeful moments, memories of the bubbles and the mountainous uprearing had surfaced in his mind and lodged there.

He casually mentioned this to the stranger.

He didn't respond, though he looked at Josh with his now customary mildness.

But Josh insisted; he felt he had the upper hand, his voice

101

cracking a little like a whip. The stranger didn't answer. He looked at Josh's face, frowning at his insistence, a new thing in him.

'Is de t'ing real?' Josh pressed. 'Or was it only somet'ing in we mind?' Josh sounded like a grownup. The stranger was amazed at how much he'd grown. One could easily mistake him for being older than he was.

No one saw the stranger for a while. No one knew where he was and Josh didn't bother to go looking for him in his hut. He told his father, 'He gaan – fo' good dis time!'

'Yuh sure, Josh?'

'Yes. Go an' see – he not dey. Even he hut not dey,' Josh said, as if he had known in advance.

'He hut not dey?' others pressed, deeply puzzled. They looked at him and at once they knew he was right.

The next night, alone, under a full April moon, Ghulam walked to the end of the village, looking everywhere for signs of the stranger's presence. He wanted proof one way or the other, he wasn't gullible any more.

But he saw nothing and continued round in a circle until his path took him back to the village. But he kept remembering the stranger's face, how their torches had crisscrossed in the night, how together they had looked into the dark face of the creek, now like an indecipherable battleground old enemies had crossed. Now, indeed, it was only memory that was left; memory like an ancient, primordial imagining that surpassed the places where they had come from – Africa, India, Europe – or where they secretly yearned to return when the soil no longer seemed to accept them; memory of a nether place, like the massacouraman itself, merely reflecting the phases of the moon where all else was vanquished or simply disappeared.

POSTSCRIPT

Hours after they left the dead one
on the brick road
the other reptiles crawled out one by one
and slowly dragged the beast back
into the creek

There they nursed him –
they tended to his wounds
they poured water out from their mouths –
they swallowed leaves
and regurgitated them onto his wounds

Slowly the beast's eyes opened
he took in the other reptiles
his eyes widened –
he remembered death, remembered the noises of people
all around him

He wondered about the water holding a mystery,
how life survived among his kind;
at once he knew prehistory and registered
everything with a splash and a commotion

which made all the others wonder
where from they actually
came

ABOUT THE AUTHOR

Cyril Dabydeen was born in the Canje district in Guyana, South America. He grew up on the Rose Hall sugar estate where he attended, and later taught at, St Patrick's Anglican School. He finished his formal education at Queen's University in Canada. He lives in Ottawa, writing and publishing with energy.

'Cyril Dabydeen is one of the most confident and accomplished voices in the Caribbean diaspora this side of the late 20th century.'
Kamau Brathwaite

ALSO BY CYRIL DABYDEEN FROM PEEPAL TREE

DISCUSSING COLUMBUS

ISBN 0-948833-57-2, 1997, £6.95

In these poems, Dabydeen explores experiences of Canada and the Caribbean which simultaneously speak of a past of brutal genocide and a world of recreating newness, constantly evolving from the heterogeneous convergencies which that voyage of 1492 began.

BERBICE CROSSING

ISBN 0-948833-69-6, 1996, £6.99

Short stories spanning the crossing between the Caribbean and North America, set variously in the urban melting pot of Toronto and the unsettling landscapes of rural Berbice with its ferocious crocodiles and even a spliff-toting Rasta.

THE WIZARD SWAMI

ISBN 0-948833-19-X, 1988, £6.99

A richly observed comedy that deals with the fate of Hindu ideals in secular and cosmopolitan Guyana as a rural Hindu teacher finds multiracial Georgetown a confusing place and discovers the dangers to religion's truths when they serve ethnic assertion.

IMAGINARY ORIGINS: SELECTED POEMS 1970-2002

ISBN 1-900715 94 5, 2004, PP. 256, £9.99

A generous selection of poems from *Goatsong*, *Distances*, *This Planet Earth*, *Heart's Frame*, *Elephant's Make Good Stepladders*, *Islands Lovelier than a Vision*, *Coastland* and other previous collections, and a dozen new poems.

Visit the Peepal Tree website and buy books online at:
www.peepaltreepress.com